Polly Samson was born in Lonc
Bed, was followed by a novel, *Oi*

For more information, visit www
Twitter: @PollySamson

'Accomplished . . . Focusing, compassionately, on apparently prosp. ...u contented people, Samson traces tremors of dis. ــ,ــىن threatening the stability of her characters' relationships and themselves' Peter Kemp, *Sunday Times*, Books of the Year

'A collection of short stories that makes you invent excuses to retire to a private place for a quick injection of reading' Bella Freud, *Evening Standard*, Books of the Year

'*Perfect Lives* links together various characters in the same town in a narrative daisy chain that allows the reader to know Samson's characters better perhaps than they know themselves. A breezy, artless writer, Samson is mercilessly accurate at lampooning middle class self-deception' *Metro*, Books of the Year

'Terrific. Funny, beautifully observed and often poignant, they're the best thing Samson has produced yet . . . This is a writer who misses nothing' Cressida Connolly, *Spectator*, Books of the Year

'These intertwined, silken stories deftly expose the heart-sickness behind so many of the burnished surfaces of contemporary life' John Banville

'Subtle and complex . . . *Perfect Lives* is an echo chamber of cause and effect, and art and life, and life and loss' Carole Cadwalladr, *Observer*

'*Perfect Lives* is beautifully structured . . . Samson is a supremely gifted prose writer. There is readiness and joy in her imagery . . . Samson sees straight through the illusions, delusions, lies, decor and outfits to her characters' weakness and hypocrisy. It makes for excellent, wincing, recognising reading' Bidisha

'Samson can be magnificently tender, caustic and thrillingly filthy all on the same page . . . . Her gaze is panoramic . . . This is a collection of delicious fondants laced with stong liquor. You can rifle through the layers, greedily consuming another story before breakfast. But the after-kick lingers for days' Liz Hoggard, *Scotsman*

'The beauty of a short story is the way in which one moment in a life can ripple outwards, offering the reader a glimpse of the past and future that surround this snapshot . . . The small intricacies of family life are

Samson's raw materials, and the stories pulse with unspoken feelings. Perhaps the greatest joy is her descriptions, often as striking and economical as poetry . . . *Perfect Lives* confirms Samson's reputation as a significant chronicler of contemporary life' Stephanie Merritt, *Observer*

'As with the finest short fiction, Polly Samson's stories show rather than tell' Boyd Tonkin, *Independent*

'Polly Samson's short stories have a light touch. They are funny too' Marianne Bruce, *Independent*

'Samson is a gifted writer with an eye for startling images' Natalie Young, *The Times*

'To describe a lyricist's prose as lyrical might almost be tautological . . . Samson excels in her lush and sensuous descriptions' Shena Mackay, *Guardian*

'Seeing what the casual observer misses, Samson exposes the underbelly of lives that on the surface appear perfect . . . All the stories are so carefully and cleverly connected that the more one reads, the more the novel-like the collection appears . . . Samson is an accomplished writer who, with this intertwined collection, has produced an original and compelling take on short fiction . . . Samson's nuanced depictions of these broken lives are moving without being sentimental, ultimately exposing "the gleam within the gloom"' Lucy Scholes, *Sunday Times*

'More than simply a series of exquisitely crafted miniatures, it encompasses many of the larger delights of a full-length novel' Sue Gaisford, *Financial Times*

'Samson is highly skilled at exploiting the overlapping fields of vision, using stray observations casually to illuminate the blind spots in others' lives . . . The shifting perspectives are matched by a suppleness of tone . . . The exactness of Samson's language and the coherence of her vision are all her own and though they conspire to make the pursuit of perfection seem a mug's game, they do it almost flawlessly' Olivia Laing, *New Statesman*

'Brilliant . . . I hesitate to call Samson's collection perfect. If it isn't perfect, it's all the better for that' Katy Guest, *Independent on Sunday*

'Polly Samson's prose is clear and precise and she makes it sparkle every now and then by producing a brilliant image . . . *Perfect Lives* has been worth the ten-year wait' Susan Hill, *Specatator*

Perfect
Lives

Also by Polly Samson

Lying in Bed

Out of the Picture

Perfect Lives

Polly Samson

virago

VIRAGO

First published in Great Britain in 2010 by Virago Press
This paperback edition published in 2011 by Virago Press

Copyright © Polly Samson 2010

The moral right of the author has been asserted.

*All characters and events in this publication, other than those
clearly in the public domain, are fictitious and any resemblance
to real persons, living or dead, is purely coincidental.*

A CIP catalogue record for this book
is available from the British Library.

ISBN 978-1-86049-993-7

Typeset in Bembo by M Rules
Printed and bound in Great Britain by
Clays Ltd, St Ives plc

Virago Press
An imprint of
Little, Brown Book Group
100 Victoria Embankment
London EC4Y 0DY

An Hachette UK Company
www.hachette.co.uk

www.virago.co.uk

For David

'It's the notion that there is no perfection – that this is a broken world and we live with broken hearts and broken lives but still that is no alibi for anything. On the contrary, you have to stand up and say hallelujah under those circumstances.'

Leonard Cohen

Contents

The Egg

Sometimes she woke to find her wedding ring on the wrong hand, but usually not. Celia Idlewild in her long chocolate dressing gown, stepping lightly down the stairs, belt tightly wound several times at the waist in the Japanese style. The coolness of stone slabs beneath her feet and faded rose damask parting with a satisfying swish on both landings, the wooden curve of the banister like silk. In the kitchen everything as it should be: black lacquer tray, two white porcelain cups, ginger thins, the Sunday morning worship just starting on the radio; gathering cereal boxes and setting them out for Ed and Laura while celestial voices soared.

Breakfast: an act of faith, for Ed and Laura rarely got up before lunch at weekends. She couldn't remember needing that much sleep when she was a teenager. She never wanted to waste the time. Fallow fields grow weeds, she says, and sets the table for them, regardless.

Bowls. Jam. Italian coffee pot on to a sputtering flame, herself on to her mat with one of her cold rosewater flannels fresh from the fridge, sliding it out of its polythene, unrolling it, lying with it cooling her eyes, fading the bruises of her dreams, and precisely twenty-five abdominal crunches, the same every day, remembering to pull up her pelvic floor with each one, taut as elastic, before her coffee percolated.

She heard the rattle of the letter box. Checked her watch. Too early for the newspaper. Glanced to the window but didn't see anyone; through the slats of the blind only great waves of grey sea reaching for the sky, curling over, collapsing, still a while to go before high tide, patches of sand still visible beyond the shingle. An empty promenade, not many gulls. She tightened the belt on her dressing gown and added the coffee pot to the tray.

Espresso coffee, ginger thins and upstairs Graham asleep beneath the eiderdown, oblivious to the sea's comings and goings, curled into his pillow, contented as the biggest brown bear should be. His back smooth, speckled across the shoulders from a summer at home, working right there at the beach with the aid of a dongle and his computer on a board across his lap, an old straw hat with a faded air-force blue band to keep the sun from giving him headaches.

Graham had done nothing to offend her from one sunny day to the next: he hadn't taken calls in another room on his mobile late at night, hadn't been to London even once – it was so much easier for him to stay in touch with his office since she'd bought him the dongle. And he'd only worn the straw hat she liked while his panama grew dusty in the cloakroom. Celia thought the blue hatband a perfect match for his eyes. With a happy sigh she added a quilted pot warmer to the tray.

Up she'd go with the tray, lose the gown, slip herself beneath that eiderdown, tuck her knees into the back of his and lie with her face to his back, arms wrapped around him, her cheek fitting along his shoulder blade like a ball in a cup, like warm clay. Just for a while she'd mould herself to his brand of warmth, to his smell: buttered toast, walnuts and bread, and the coffee in its pot hot for a while yet.

She checked the front door as she passed with the tray to see if by some happy miracle the newspapers had arrived and almost dropped it, hot coffee and all, on to the floor when she saw what was waiting for her there. She had to put the tray on the hall table and take a closer look: it was disgusting what some people would do.

She could see at once what it was, spreading itself over the stones like a stain, split yolk spilling a gob of a sunset, a nacreous sea, oh God, and someone had written something on the shell. Celia could see a few letters still intact. Someone had posted this egg through the letter box with a message. So, not mindless hooliganism then. For a few soft and carefree moments, Celia could not imagine who would do such a thing. Then, as the swan's down blew away and it dawned on her who might, she had to turn around and check that there was no one coming down the stairs to witness her outrage.

For once she was glad that her children were happy to sleep their lives away and she was the lone early riser; even Graham slept the sleep of the blameless and never stirred before coffee.

For a moment she was puzzled by what was written on

the egg. HAPPY FAT. But not for long. She felt suddenly quite shaken and had to sit down on the stairs.

What a revolting thing to do! She stood again and bent closer to the broken egg. Its shell was pale brown. A full half remained capsized in a sea of gloop. Celia's stomach turned at the sight of it. There were capital letters in what appeared to be black pen. HAPPY FAT. The rest of the message was lost in smithereens of shell that smattered in the slime.

Celia hated eggs almost as much as she hated eggshell. She hadn't eaten anything eggy, not even meringues, since she was forced to as a child, though she sometimes, very kindly in her opinion, boiled them for Graham and the children: stripy blue and white egg cups, buttered toast cut into soldiers, nicely done and set before them without a word. Yolks burst as they plunged in, dribbled over jagged shells, bits of gritty salt sticking to slippery blind whites. Graham insisting they smash the shells with their spoons: an Idlewild family tradition, he said, to stop the witches using them as boats in which to sail out to sea and sink ships. Then came the crunch of the spoons on the shells. The wooden stools at the breakfast counter ranged so they all faced straight out to sea. From every window the Idlewilds could watch the waves that would bear the witches along; the sound of the weather came to them first and the ancient sashes rattled with rumours.

The wanton devastation of those eggshells among the surviving soldiers and crusts made Celia gag every time and she wished her family would eat porridge instead, or let the witches have their boats. There were shards of eggshell in her mouth, stuck for ever in the careless scrambled eggs that her mother made, the unexpected crunch of it and it sticking against her throat and lodging in the bite surfaces of her molars so she'd keep finding its grittiness along with buttery scrambled egg as she was made to chew: 'Oh don't make such a fuss Celia, just swallow', but Celia couldn't swallow.

She looked back up the stairs quickly to check there was still no one coming. She thought she heard a door opening, so shot to the kitchen for a cloth. Normally she would wear rubber gloves for anything involving a dishcloth but on the occasion of the egg she couldn't wait to get the mess off the floor and out of sight. Away into a carrier bag, cloth and all, knotted in the way people do when disposing of nappies, and deep into the bin.

She sat at the table and started working her way through the pot of coffee alone. The egg had reduced the crystalline possibility of her morning to slime. The domed shell of it in that smear of sunset; the crispy sound of it crushing inside the dishcloth as she closed her fist. Slime and shell. Egg bomb. Stink bomb. Bombshell.

Sometimes too much caffeine could bring on an annoying twitch, just the outer corner of her right eye. Look quick. Outside the sea rose in foam and dashed itself on to the shore. In a dark grey sky white gulls battled the wind. Not, then, the sort of day that should bring a visitor to the coast.

Celia used to watch her twitch in the mirror. Graham claimed he couldn't see it when she tried to get him to notice. He wasn't quick enough: blink and you miss it. Tickety tic. His eyes slid away, back beneath the brim of his hat. Not nervy like her. Steady and kind so he'd hate to think that he'd been the one to put the tic in there. She'd always been quick to flinch, like a horse that was easily spooked. She gulped the last of the coffee, feeling it hit her insides. Shut her eyes.

Graham upstairs in bed. She'd take up coffee. The tray on the floor, him turning on to his back. Through the window, despite the bad weather, three kitesurfers galloping over the waves, powerful backs and legs hinging up and down like well-oiled machinery and Graham's strong hands keeping her steady, sails billowing, rising and falling, crashing and skimming.

But the egg. Her fingers tapped the work surface as a sermon on the radio reached its happy conclusion. It was, as these things so often are, about forgiveness and she hadn't listened to a word of it. No point crying over a broken egg, she told herself. The whole family together and people for lunch later. A good leg of lamb and white peaches for Bellinis beforehand.

She thought about starting again: a fresh pot of coffee, maybe squeezing some oranges. She summoned up a picture, one of her favourites: Graham, from the early days. The fading light of the Idlewilds' garden, running away from him between dark green hedges of clipped box, a summer's night.

'Come here and let me kiss you', and skitting away across the lawn, laughing. Allowing him to catch her, and pretending to struggle as he kissed her. Holding hands, she in the loveliest yellow cotton dress, the belt was like a daisy chain. Him pulling her to an octagon of lawn in the furthest reach of the Idlewilds' jewel-box garden, a scented paradise wrought even lovelier by time. The setting sun gilding their limbs and flowers overflowing like baubles, glowing hypnotically against the green of the hedges. Impossibly tall hollyhocks, shimmery-stemmed, silver leaves of artemesia and roses, roses, roses, geraniums and lilies, rubies, garnets and pearls.

'Kiss me back or I'll bite you,' he said, growling into her ear, backing her against the only tree, a golden russet with rusty leaves and fruit as hard and round as little brass knobs. She let him bite her neck.

'Kiss me and I'll tell you a secret.'

'Never,' she said, turning her face away.

'Something I've never told anyone before.

'We never eat the fruit from this tree, by the way,' he said, looking up into its branches, keeping his knee pressing her against its trunk. He held her arms above her head: 'I think you'd better promise me you won't,' he said as sternly as he could muster. He could make her promise him anything just by kissing her.

She could feel the bark against the backs of her hands and through the leaves two marble statues, their heads turned towards the tree: Adam and Eve, garlands falling from their hair, blind eyes beseeching.

'OK.' She laughed. 'I won't eat the fruit if you tell me your secret', and he blew a little warm air into her ear.

'Do you think we'll get a chance to you-know-what while we're here?' she said. 'Will they really make me sleep in the tower room on my own?' He kissed her.

'OK, a secret,' he said when the kissing was done, though his knee stayed where it made her ache. 'It's about Eve.' He nodded to the statue. Eve stared reproachfully back at them from her pedestal.

'Something I've never told anyone before.' The serpent had been carved winding up Eve's leg, its head reached rather suggestively beyond her knee. She was four feet tall, five with her pedestal, naked but for a fig leaf, an apple in the upturned marble fingers of her right hand.

'It's such pure white stone,' Celia said, trying not to let it show that she could barely speak as he brushed his lips along her neck. No one had ever had this effect on her before.

'Is it English?' she managed to squeak. She had a vague recall of something from her art history course in Florence. Didn't all the best marble come from Italy in the eighteenth century?

Graham let go of her and sprang away. He stood, grinning at her from behind Eve. His hands covered the statue's breasts and Celia felt a spiteful jolt that took her by surprise.

'I used to love her bare bosoms when I was a boy,' he said, laughing, pretending to tenderly caress them until she felt that she would like to kick the statue over. 'Sometimes, in the holidays, she was the first thing I'd think of when I got home.'

Celia stuck her tongue out at him. 'Well, I rather fancy Adam,' she retorted. And then, wildly for her because she rarely let down her guard, she threw herself at the hideously veined feet of the Adam statue and knelt, kissed his knees, then his bulging thighs and finally aimed her mouth at his well-placed marble fig leaf.

'Mmmmm, mmmmmm, mmmmm,' she mimed, with her lips to the cold stone.

'Celia!'

'Mmmmmmm', as though her mouth was full.

'Celia!' said Graham again, but with greater urgency.

She moaned louder still, pretending to pull Adam closer, her hands running up and down the cold ridges of his stomach.

'Celia! Stop!' Graham hissed, but still it took her far too long to register that standing there, along with the elderly local doctor and his wife, were Graham's parents, all four affecting coughs. 'Ah, yes, musk roses,' his mother was saying, fluttering her hand at her chest.

'Commissioned by my grandfather . . .' Graham's father told her, completely deadpan, 'because he thought this place was like Eden.' While she smoothed down her skirt: 'Well, it is like Paradise,' she said, chattering, holding out her hand to be shaken, 'all the flowers and the lovely grass and the view, and yes, hello, it's very nice to meet you, too.'

'They're going to love you! I can tell,' Graham said after they'd been left alone, tactfully but not without tangible reproach, together in Adam and Eve's garden, but Celia knew that she would never be lovely in their eyes. Despite becoming the provider of two unimpeachably marvellous grandchildren, she was always a little bit the slattern in the yellow dress who came up for the weekend from London, shocked the natives, fellated their statue and won their only son.

In my perfect life: a song on the car radio, a dark brown voice that they both liked. The roof peeled back, her head-scarf tied like Grace Kelly, or so she thought at the time.

'In my perfect life my son won't go to boarding school. When we have a son I want him home by the fire.' Another trip later that summer, her in the same yellow dress, Graham at the wheel of his beloved MG Midget.

'*In my perfect life I don't mind playing the fool . . .*' They sang along to the chorus, they could both sing in tune, her voice slotted naturally a perfect octave above his: '*In my perfect life there's you, you, you. And no matter what you do I will always love you. In my perfect life . . .*' and then Graham changing the words and looking straight at her, singing over whatever it was in the song, '*. . . and my daughters will all look like you.*'

Celia remembered the directness of his smile, the shape of it: lips almost like a handle hanging from a deep dimple in each cheek. Nowadays those dimples were lost to a pair of creases running all the way from the corners of his eyes. In brackets was how she thought of his smile now. And those air-force blue eyes! How delicious it'd been when he'd turned them on her that day to sing to her, as she hugged herself beneath the car blanket, legs tucked up and radiating warmth and happiness like a broody hen.

She hugged herself through her dressing gown as she remembered. That lovely yellow dress. Standing together for a while in the octagonal garden, the black darts of swallows and house martins ticking across a sky that was streaked in silvery layers of pearl and mauve, like the inside of a shell. The dress undone. Nuzzling the crook of his arm.

Celia rose from the table and slid her hand inside her gown where the warmth of her left breast was a comfort. At the window she peered through the slats of the blinds. Already there were more people about. Men crouched Neanderthally over their metal detectors along the shore. Early birds to the worm. The first joggers and the dogs brought to shit on the beach.

Every morning Celia began her day the same way.

Called to attention by the window, its sashes shaken by the onshore wind, usually more than a breeze. She gazed out at the beach as she invariably did, trying to hook her eyes to the sea all the way to the horizon and not to let them fall on the litter blowing about across the shingle, the scavengers, the shitting dogs. Three men in wheelchairs often stopped for a while in front of the house, not through any choice of their own; stargazers brought for the air, catching her attention. Always one man in particular, when he was there. Neck twisting like a corkscrew, head tipped back, a full head of dark hair and a clean padded black anorak. Long arms and legs; lips, shiny red and wet as sea anemones, open. Once, out on the pavement, she heard the sounds that he made, the baby-cry and yodel of it all and when she passed she saw the wedding ring, loose on his pale finger, and started to weep. Him with his head turned to the sky but looking elsewhere, maybe having a dream, hair being blown about, hard to say if he liked the sea air or not. Too awful if he didn't. Never his wife. Always one of the men in green care-home uniforms pushing his chair to a standstill, like a barrow of fruit, in front of her window. She stood the second pot of coffee on the tray. The same stretch of beach every morning, green painted railings, caramel-coloured shingle, stones and shale thrown carelessly on to the groynes.

The same stretch of beach, their house new to them then: 'Yes, we're incredibly lucky with the position,' and she'd so carefully laid out the party between the groynes, all those candles and flags of years ago. Graham's birthday: tables and chairs, lilies in glass fishbowls, so much expense and trouble. Crystal and linen, not plastic partyware. Thinking at the time that they'd have many more.

Billowing windbreaks made with long wooden poles and dazzling white cotton sheets. The bleached lace tablecloths weighted down with stones from the beach. She had candles in jars, some hanging from long bamboo canes wedged into the stones, and plates piled high with tiger prawns, hot chilli dip, dressed crab, French bread and cheese that had to be eaten with a spoon. The oyster man was on hand to shuck the oysters, wearing a striped apron. There was lean roast beef and potato salad, bottles lodged in silver buckets of ice. There was a birthday cake, candles. Celia suddenly found herself craving a cigarette. Instead she set about clearing up the old coffee grounds, using the side of her hand to push them on top of the plastic bag that contained the egg mess. The forty golden birthday candles were never lit.

'So would you press the red button then?' A handsome young dandy who'd been brought along, a friend of a friend. He was wearing a waistcoat that looked like it was made out of gold foil, and eyeing her suggestively as he took a swig from the neck of his beer. He said he wanted to know if she'd push a hypothetical red button that would make all her dreams come true if it meant exterminating an anonymous Chinaman in the process.

'No one would know you'd done it,' he said, now quite openly flirting, running his knuckles along her arm. 'I wouldn't tell anyone.'

'But all my dreams have already come true,' said Celia, laughing, pulling her arm away to gesture up at her house standing tall and creamily-stuccoed above the beach like a lone tooth.

A woman in tight jeans scrunched towards them across the stones, talking to Graham. Bright lipstick, shoes too high for the beach but rather than take them off like everyone else she had to keep hanging off Graham to steady herself.

'This way for cold beer,' he said, introducing the bucket of ice and Celia in one wave of his arm. 'Or maybe champagne, thanks to my beautiful wife.'

'Beautiful wife' – he always knew when to reassure her. 'This is Celia,' he said. 'And this, Rachel. You may have met before.'

'I don't think so,' said Celia. 'But maybe.' The flirtatious man with the hypothetical red button offered to open some champagne to wash down the oysters.

'I'm not sure we've met before either, but I did set eyes on your gorgeous daughter yesterday morning,' said Rachel, claiming her attention. There was lipstick on two of her incisors. 'What a sweetie! Watching her in her Connaught House uniform! So little with that great big satchel! Bobbing up and down on the end of Graham's arm.'

'What?' said Celia, about to laugh. The man in the foil waistcoat was being comically inept with the champagne bottle. He had it wedged between his knees.

'Yes, I stopped at the crossing. I hadn't realised that you had one so young.'

Graham had gone puce.

'Our daughter goes to school down the road from here, not London,' said Celia. 'She goes on the bus.'

'It wasn't me,' he said.

'Oh yes, you were wearing your long dark green coat, and . . .'

Celia stared at him. He was like a beetroot beneath the cream panama; a proper Borsalino it was, they'd bought it together in Milan at Easter. She would never find him handsome in a panama again.

'Don't you remember? I waved,' Rachel continued, as though now she'd started she couldn't stop. She seemed to have become swept up, for she couldn't have missed the tempest in Celia's blue eyes. It takes just one thing: a freak in the weather; a bit of a rage; a tsunami snatching people up from the shore like jacks in its giant fist; a thermal mael-strom; the wrong sneeze; the bad geography where tectonic plates rub themselves into a frenzy; or a Rachel at a party who can casually shatter a perfect life with a few words.

'Hey, Mum.' Ed came into the kitchen and stood with her at the window. A man in a tracksuit was at the railings swinging several dog leads. The man in the chair had been wheeled away.

'He's got really shitty dogs,' Ed said knowledgeably, yawning, scratching under his T-shirt.

'What are you doing out of bed this early?' Celia reached up to feel his forehead, to get a breath of him. Ed at sev-enteen, his father's smile: out in the open, just happy, not in brackets. Hair unbrushed, sticking up all over, stripy pyjama bottoms with the T-shirt, making him look like her little boy all over again.

'Laura and I *were* planning to bring you and Dad break-fast in bed,' he said, wagging his finger. 'But you always get up so early, so it'll just be Dad.' He scowled at the door. 'But Laura's still not awake.' He sighed. 'I've told her it's Father's Day three times already. I'll have to go and pour water into her ear.'

16

Celia took the second pot off the tray and poured herself another cup; so what if she started to shake.

'*What have you done?*' Celia masking her scream while that Rachel woman prattled on. Her own voice a hiss and the horrible silence when Graham didn't answer. The Rachel in her tight jeans looking from one to the other, still confused, stupid woman, and then looking swiftly away. Little Ed and littler Laura running along the groynes to join the party. Laura's blonde hair flying behind her, Ed punching the air, leaping, glad to be at the sea on a summer's evening, stones flying up as they ran, the pair of them as joyous and sleek as porpoises in bright water.

Ed clattered back into the kitchen, followed by Laura in her unflattering pyjamas; still her same darling porpoises but bigger. Impossibly bigger: Ed's rugby physique; Laura's milkmaid beauty of the kind that makes you expect to see laced corsets and dimples. Out of the window the sun hit the waves, blades of steel flashing and slicing and the daredevil kitesurfers still going strong. Celia turned from the view, away from the sad tidings and the hum of the pavement sweeper along the promenade. She could feel the twitch start up beneath her eye as Ed and Laura started the noisy business of making smoothies, the buzz saw of the blender and asking her how many minutes to set the timer so they'd be soft: eggs for their father, though Celia wished they wouldn't, reaching to the shelf for a pill, always bird-like between her two children, sharper than she thinks she should be. But what big frames teenagers all had these days. Probably the good nutrition. Even the girls: it wasn't unusual for them to have size eleven feet. Something of the dairy about the lot of them, especially the noise a whole herd could make clonking around the place like heifers.

The letter box rattled. 'The newspaper.' Ed scraped back his stool.

'No, let me,' Celia pushed past him, 'I'll get it.' What if there were to be another egg? And another? A dozen? She rested a hand on the door jamb to steady herself.

On the beach, the children told to stay inside, all the guests gone. Ed and Laura's little faces peaky at the high window like workhouse orphans. In the morning nothing left of the party but ragged remnants of the white sheets obscenely strewn like old shrouds on to the shingle, still attached to the snapped windbreak poles. Nothing left of the flowers or the cake or the dressed crabs that she'd smashed into the seething foam. Everything gone, most of it snatched by a sea that grew hungrier and wilder until it roared hard enough to drown out his voice. Everything gone except the rented tables and chairs but by morning they had gone too, stolen by two men with a trailer.

They'd seen the men drive off. Silently sitting side by side on the balcony, watching the tide melt away, the empty beach, a slight pinkening at the edge of the sky.

'I will stay with you if you promise to never see that child again.' Celia watching the wind pull at a scrap of fabric, bits of white sheet flapping up and down like the wing of a dying bird.

'If you do see it, I will divorce you. I mean it.' Both apple and snake in one hiss.

The surprising thing to Celia was that she did mean it and she meant it again and again as her rage was brought back to her by tides that came bearing cruel souvenirs from

18

that night. Once Celia found a birthday candle still attached to its cup washed up on the stones. The plastic holder had been worn white but the candle was still partly golden.

It was only the newspaper and not another egg waiting for her by the front door. She inhaled deeply but the long sigh that was to follow stalled in her throat. She heard the rattle of the tray, Ed's voice. Ed and Laura started up the stairs ahead of her. 'Coming, Mum?'

'In a minute.'

She went back to the kitchen and looked out at the beach. A girl was standing alone holding the rails, looking out to sea, her long fair hair blown in ribbons about her head. Celia thought again of the flirtatious young man in his fabulous foil waistcoat, his fingers on her arm: 'Go on, push it. You know you want to.'

She looked back to the girl, hair whipping out, jeans and grey sweatshirt, no coat. About the right age. She imagined the girl turning around. A face she might know in an instant if she opened the door. Would she open the door?

'Would you press the red button?' His hand on her arm. He'd had the most bewitching smile, very bright teeth. Would she? She swallowed hard, waiting for a while, almost willing the girl to be the one and then, picking up the newspaper, wondered that she wouldn't welcome the intrusion.

Barcarolle

Richard lowered the lid of his piano as gently as a man closing a coffin and lingered for a moment, his fingers resting on the polished wood and a slight stoop to his back that was almost a bow. Lunch took him a couple of minutes: two slices of watery ham laid to rest between two of bread and butter and a tall glass of water from the tap, before shrugging himself into the dark blue waterproof that he refused to think of as an anorak. He pulled its collar to the wind and loped down his front steps sideways, keeping his back to the weather.

The black Mini, neatly parked at the kerb, made an unlikely partner for such a long-striding man. Behind the wheel he was cramped like something about to hatch. He had to force himself to scrabble his fingers into the disgusting ashtray for parking change. He'd almost kicked the smoking again. It helped that he'd never mastered the art of playing the piano and smoking at the same time.

Cigarettes and driving, though, that was different: he could satisfy his nicotine cravings with ease so his car smelled, as usual, like a sticky Sunday morning hangover. It was all part of the punishment, that bad atmosphere, like keeping the change in the ashtray. He never really had passengers so there was no one else to care.

Nothing but coppers and old fag ash in there. He cursed as he got out of the car and the gulls swore back at him. The wind brought salt to his lips and he wound a thick scarf around his neck. It was a good warm scarf, a recent present to himself, with wide stripes of yellow and black, almost like the one he'd worn all through college. He should walk. Really, it would do him good. He checked the car door by rattling its handle a couple of times and ambled downhill along the cracked kerb, reciting quietly to himself the names of the people he had promised to visit that afternoon: 'Hammonds at Marine Parade, then Anna Something-or-other, 29 Evrika Street, and then,' he managed a smile at the last, 'five o'clock, the Idlewilds.'

A vision of the Idlewild family, all four glossy heads bent like new conkers around their golden and glowing grand piano came floating into his head. It was a Bösendorfer concert piano of such perfection that the mere thought of it stopped him feeling quite so grumpy at having to leave the flat and his own dear piano and, in particular, the Chopin Barcarolle that had held him within its bittersweet embrace for the last week and four days and four nights.

Chopin's late-flowering masterpiece. His step lightened as he embellished the already sublime image of the Idlewilds and their heavenly piano with a vision of himself, at its keys, sleeves of his black polo neck thrust to his elbows, head thrown back, not only confident but magnificent, playing for them and them alone Chopin's one and only Barcarolle.

He crossed Crescent Place, letting his eyes stretch beyond the estate agents and the carpet shop and down the street to the esplanade with its bright green railings and the churning dirtier green of the sea beyond. He was well prepared, as it happened. His performance of the lovely piece was almost as perfect as it would ever be: practically concert standard.

He kept heading seawards, Chopin keeping time with his step and the architecture becoming grander: creamy plasterwork more ornate, curlicues and pillars, houses like wedding cakes looming six storeys, some more.

Tuning pianos took him more often than not to this more decorative part of town. Fancy iron balconies and lofty views out to sea. It was almost high tide. He saw the rescue boat being launched, bellying into the waves in pursuit of some fool or other.

It was the extra humidity that did for pianos, and one as grand as the Idlewilds' Bösendorfer must never be allowed to fall out of tune. Richard made it his duty to attend to it often. The thought of it shimmering, toned and tuned to perfection, upped the tempo of his step still more and he swung the leather case of tuning tools as he carried on along the promenade, now no more or less happy than anyone else he passed.

The Barcarolle that had been occupying him was playing out in the peaks and troughs and in the trilling ripples of the waves: Chopin's ornamental genius in full bloom; grace notes aplenty. Though this Barcarolle had been the despair of many an artist, Richard hadn't expected to find it quite so frustrating to master himself. Twenty-odd years ago it had seemed effortless for some exam or other.

He reached 7 Marine Parade where Mrs Hammond, or Morganna, as she had insisted early on in his tender relationship with her family's piano he was to call her, was waiting for him at the shiny black door, a slinky Burmese cat snaking around her bare legs. Morganna: eyes ringed dramatically with kohl, like a slightly raddled Cleopatra. Always a bit too much of an eyeful. 'Grotrian Steinweg,' he reminded himself as she shut the door, bracelets jingling. 'Glossy black lacquered case, in need of toning.'

'Oh, you look freezing, are you sure you won't have a cup of tea?' Morganna asked, hugging herself and shivering slightly, breasts pointy through her sweater, as though she were the one who'd just come in from the cold.

Morganna's piano was imprisoned in a shockingly purple room that she referred to, with a self-deprecating snort, as 'the library'. It had many more random objects lying about than actual books: an elaborate and dusty music stand, an equally dusty cello, a rather panicked-looking rocking horse. Opposite the piano a collection of marionettes were hanging from the gallows of a hat stand, a captive audience in various states of strangulation; and a parrot, a large green one with ketchup-coloured markings, who screamed mutinous threats at such pitch whenever Richard came to tune the piano that he had finally spoken up and asked Morganna to remove it. It threw sunflower seeds at him as he passed.

'I've got psittacosis, I've got psittacosis,' squawked Morganna in a horribly accurate approximation of the parrot and it clung furiously to the bars as she picked up its cage. It turned its head at an acutely ugly angle, appraising him from beneath its red eyelids, not liking what it saw, then started to hiss, not quite imperceptibly, which Richard found almost worse than its shrieking.

'He never speaks at all when you're here,' Morganna said, pouting a little, and she swung from the room to make the cup of tea that he didn't really want with the cat at her heels, the brass cage hanging from her arm and the parrot's pitch and volume so piercing that it made his ears hurt.

Before he could get to work, however, he still had many twisty candelabra and silver-framed family photographs to deal with. He started evicting them from the top of the piano, piling Morganna and Co. face down on to an arm-chair with all the tenderness of a man stacking bricks. If this piano were his he'd rather die than cover it in such detritus. Whatever would he put there anyway? Not pictures of his family – he shuddered slightly at the thought – and certainly not the school portraits they displayed with the bone-china shepherdesses on a table at home, so prominently that anyone would think they were still proud of him. Those un-modest moments caught against the sky-blue backdrop, the smart parting (he could still feel the tooth of the headmistress's comb along a line of his scalp), the blinding flash of the photographer's bulb and him always pulling the same expression: lips turned down in an effort not to brag but eyes telling a different story as he cradled the silver cup. Same photo year after year until they decided to let some whiney girl and her violin win.

He glared at a picture of Morganna, smiling up at him, her head wreathed in jasmine. What a prize she'd been.

'What do you think it is, a sideboard?' he muttered to the freshly-sprigged bride. There was no point getting so annoyed. Morganna's teeth looked like a toothpaste commercial; her hair sleek as liquorice on her wedding day.

As if the full weight of the family's most photogenic moments were not enough, the piano was covered by a piece of tapestry with annoying tassels that swung like sheep's daggles as he pulled it away to throw over the pictures. Only then could he lift the lid and fit the prop stick into place.

The golden strings shone inside like a harp and he hoped that there'd be a little stolen time after the tuning to let it sing with his Barcarolle. He laid out his tool roll, the bits and pieces side by side; like a child again, sharpening pencils before an exam, hammers and wrenches all within reach – and then, just as Morganna and her amorous cat appeared with his tea, he noticed the damage: a nasty gash right on the shiny black front of the piano. His heart missed a beat. It was a wishbone-sized injury, where the cheek met the lid, and deep enough to be down to the palest wood at the centre.

'Ahh.' Morganna reappeared, saw him with his finger fixed to the wound, as though attempting to stem its bleeding. A small splutter, she clearly hadn't meant to laugh; he looked round and saw her bite her lip.

'Lola, last night. Total temper tantrum, I'm afraid. Threw a candlestick . . . don't think she meant to hit the piano, at least I hope she didn't . . .' Her voice faltered when he didn't speak.

The wood felt rough and splintery. This Grotrian, he now remembered, had a particularly lustrous top end.

'. . . All I'd asked her to do was ten minutes' practice on her lovely Nocturne . . .' Ten minutes, he thought, what's the point of that?

He tapped his tuning fork on his knee and clenched it between his teeth, making his head buzz; he pressed middle A on the piano; listened for the synchronisation of the beats; dismissed her. Well flat.

'I always tell them how much they'll regret giving up. I know I did,' said Morganna to the cat. 'Ten minutes' practice a day, that's all I've ever asked of them.'

Luckily Morganna didn't seem to need a response because the lawful wedded cat was purring so loudly that he knew he'd have to wait for them to leave before he could start the tuning proper.

Again he tapped the tuning fork – *ten minutes'* practice a day – and held it vibrating in his teeth. His own father threatened to dock his pocket money if he didn't *stop* practising – 'Out you go, make some friends. For Christ's sake go tickle something other than the ivories' – always insisting that he took the dog, a foul-breathed cocker spaniel called Jasper for walks. The thing he really couldn't stand about Jasper was that when Jasper shook his head his stinky drool flew everywhere.

His father, always hinting at a world beyond the piano. That time after his performance at the Wigmore Hall: 'Don't you think it's time you went out and got yourself laid?' So vulgar; as though getting laid would have done a thing to prevent the shaking of his hands; as though getting laid would have helped him become reattached to the pair of pale flounders which had just slithered their way over the keys of the Wigmore Hall's Steinway, leaving him flummoxed and drowning. Fish-fingered. Useless hands floundered.

He pleated a strip of green felt between the central section of strings and tried not to dwell. His father's face so hideous whenever he talked about sex: 'Don't you think it's time you got yourself laid?' Lips too wet. Another occasion so inappropriately remarking on the breasts of Aurelia Lieberman, and licking his lips in a way that brought Jasper the dog to mind. After that he'd felt slightly sick every time he sat a masterclass with Aurelia Lieberman in the tight pearl-grey jumper that she wore.

It took Richard just over an hour to reach the pragmatic compromise that equal temperament tuning demanded. Even if the gods were not happy, Morganna and her family should be, and he let loose with a flourish of chromatics. Perfectly spaced semitones rang out across the shambled room: crystalline, clean as peppermint. The piano was wasted on this family. He'd make time to loosen things up with the Chopin, if Morganna would only leave him alone, and then it'd be just the unknown piano in Evrika Street to get out of the way before he could throw himself before the majesty of that Bösendorfer. He straightened up for a moment to relieve the ringing in his ears and was irritated to hear a squawk from the parrot.

It had been the tightly-sweatered Ms Lieberman who had recommended him for the Haydn recital at the Wigmore Hall but she hadn't turned up to meet him on the day, like she said she would. Hours before concert time, his palms sweating; wiping them on the pocket lining of the tails that his father had just shelled out for.

Then, too close to the start, his father in his dressing

room: 'So, where's Aurelia, then?' As though she was somehow part of the deal, and his mother standing behind
looking too bright-eyed in a new turquoise dress that didn't
suit her, and for the second time his father's sleazy baritone:
'Is Aurelia coming, or not?' Don't lick your lips like that.
Dirty dog. Please don't lick your lips. He wasn't sure he
hadn't said it aloud: Don't lick your lips like that, Dogface.
His pockets were wringing wet. He was shaking his head
like a madman, trying to expel the image of his father's
slobbery maw when he took to the stage, tails of the new
jacket flying.

He must have spent longer at the Grotrian than he'd
intended. The light was already burnishing the waves when
he left Morganna's. He checked his watch: this next piano
could take an age and he didn't want to be late for the
Idlewilds. The woman, Anna, hadn't seemed too certain
about anything much when she called, except to say that it
was an upright. Sometimes he wished he'd never taken out
the advert that gave every Tom, Dick and Anna his phone
number. Her house at 29 Evrika Street was a walk into
wind away from Marine Parade but at least it took him east,
which was the right direction for that Bösendorfer.

He had been tuning the Idlewilds' piano for over a
decade. It was about as perfect as such an old and well
attended to friend could be: twenty tons of exquisite ten-
sion, he quickened his step at the thought of it, held like
a drawn bow inside gleaming rosewood. From the first
moment he had touched a note, that heavenly piano had
resonated in a very tender part of his heart. Angels sang
there. 1920s Vienna had indeed been a golden age for
pianos. The first time he'd laid his fingers on its keys its

gracious harmonics rang out, a full dozen tones, suspended in the air at his will.

But first Evrika Street. He turned into Anna's road with the wind gusting at his back.

She ushered him out of the cold afternoon, chattering: 'It was my brother Leo who was the musical one. When he gave up the piano my parents let it go to my cousins', and into the steam of her kitchen, in time to whip a huge rattling saucepan off the cooker. This Anna's kitchen was ablaze with colour but it was her hands that he noticed first, hands that moved with a quick grace among the reds and yellows and oranges and bright blues. She looked slightly windswept, breathless, hair falling around her face, pushing it back with long fingers, ink-stained at their tips so he found himself staring, explaining that she'd only recently got the piano so it wasn't because she was stupid that she hadn't been able to answer all of his technical questions about it on the telephone. Smiling ruefully as she said: 'I wouldn't know what a fixed soundboard was if you hit me over the head with it,' and reaching for some large wooden tongs to fish about in the steaming aluminium pan, she swirled fabric around in bubbling purple dye that looked like a sorcerer's brew, still talking.

'But it has crossed an ocean, so I thought I should find the best tuner I could and your name came up. Sorry about this,' she said, gesturing at the pan and pouring a fountain of salt from a paper bag into the potion. 'I'll be able to leave it to do its thing in a minute,' she continued; glancing up at him through the steam. He watched her long arms, pointed elbows showing beneath her baggy sleeves. Tall, but slight, she was what he supposed people meant by gamine. He liked her fleeting smile, the uncertainty of it, the way that it still managed to light her whole face. He didn't mind standing there looking at her at all.

'I do textiles,' she said, fixing a lid to the saucepan and sweeping an arm to introduce the swathes and bolts of bright fabrics that until then he'd only peripherally taken in. 'I'm constantly dyeing.' Colours swagged and stretched and hung like flags over the backs of the chairs, looping across the cupboards in dazzling blues and oranges like the sails of some fabulous boat.

'I like to wash my hands before a tuning,' he said, turning them palms up. A little of the dye had splashed above her top lip, leaving two small purple freckles that he longed to wipe away with the tip of his finger. She opened a door off the hall and he saw it was regatta time in there, too. Strips and streamers in storm-blues and mauves hung in clumps like particularly beautiful seaweed from a Sheila Maid hitched over the bath. As their shoulders touched at the narrow door the bulb blew with such a sudden ping that they both jumped.

She was up on the chair changing the bulb. She was balancing with one leg bent, the other foot resting along her shin. She put him in mind of an Anglepoise lamp. Or a flamingo. Her jumper was pink. It lifted as she raised her arm to remove the shade. He saw the disconcerting curve of her waist and the small muscles moving along the bottom of her spine as she pressed her long bare foot back to the seat of the chair to balance.

'I really resented not being the musical one learning the piano,' she said, screwing in the new bulb. Her skin was smooth, polished walnut. There was something about the unexpected sight of her backbone that reminded him of dampers along strings and he was relieved when the bulb was in place and she lowered her arm so the jumper settled back at the waistband of her jeans. She jumped down and switched on the light. A noisy fan that compensated for the lack of window started to whirr. He cleared his throat.

'It wasn't so easy being the musical one, actually,' he said, pausing with the soap in his hands. 'The day some music teacher told my parents that I had perfect pitch it was like they'd won the pools,' and his words, in her small bathroom, hit his own ears, whether through the distortion of the fan or the strangeness of having such a conversation, like he was listening to someone else on the radio.

'I couldn't understand what was going on when I got home from school. Big pat on the back, as though I'd scored a goal. Champagne, even. What on earth did they think was going to happen next?'

He started flicking water from his fingers into the basin and Anna handed him a towel. 'Later on I had to look up the word "prodigy" in the dictionary and it frightened the life out of me,' he said, drying his hands.

Anna leaned against the towel rail, again that smile. 'Prodigy,' she said, brushing her fringe from her eyes, 'how wonderful', and blood rushed to his cheeks.

'The thing is there's always someone more gifted,' he said in a fluster, the fan still whirring. 'It doesn't matter how hard you work, there's always someone who can do it better with less effort. There was this guy, Leszek, at college with me. Ahh . . .' His voice really did seem to have taken on a life of its own. It went stumbling on.

'. . . I would sweat over a piece for weeks and then this

Leszek would saunter over to the practice room and wouldn't be able to help himself but sit down and play my piece quite effortlessly, whatever it happened to be.' Leszek Smolsky had also owned a strangely boxy and black Russian camera, another thing. 'He could do whatever he turned his mind to.' His grainy low-lit photographs were moody like stills from French films.

'What a show-off,' said Anna. Her eyes were greyish and her gaze direct when she used her forearm to hold the hair back from her face. The purple freckles were delicate; they looked like beauty spots.

'The thing is, he came from Poland and no one could even hate him for being so bloody good because he'd been taken away from his family at the age of five and plonked in an academy where he played for a minimum of eight hours every day, birthdays included, for the next twenty years before finding his way to the Guild.' Leszek's relentless charisma: his black and white portraits of some of the college's female students made it appear that their fortunes lay not in their musicality but in their physiques. 'Everyone felt sorry for him,' Richard said, though that wasn't strictly true. 'Apart from me, that is: I'd have loved his life.' Anna laughed and he found himself flexing his fingers over an imaginary keyboard and taking a modest bow.

'Born in the wrong country, wrong regime, Comrade,' she said, smiling at him again. 'Poor you, though it could've been worse, you could have been born in the wrong family, like me. I screamed when the piano was taken away but no one took a blind bit of notice because I wasn't the "musical one".' She looked down at her interlaced inky fingers then stretched them, still linked, over her head. She pulled a comic face, lips in a downward clown, that didn't really convince.

'You were the "artistic one", then, were you?' He gestured to the great loops and ribbons twirling from the ceiling.

'No, that was my sister Tilda.' She laughed again. 'And my other brother was the "clever one". I was the "kind one".' Her voice *was* kind, come to think of it, and it had a lovely sad lilt to it. He wondered where she was from. 'Sounds like a consolation prize, doesn't it?' Behind her the colourful streamers danced to the beat of the fan.

'Shall I show you the piano?' she said, softly breaking the spell.

He could tell with one glance that Anna's piano was a lost cause. It stood against the wall of a small sitting room like an old bore. There were velvet armchairs and a fat sofa but Richard's eyes were immediately drawn to the floor, where a last stripe of light from the window was falling on to a glorious and intricate rug that seemed to ripple against the boards. It was blazing, iridescent: all the colours of sunset and sea.

'That's a beauty,' he said, at the same time as she opened the lid of her piano. Seeing her face light up he realised that she might think he was talking about the piano, which was anything but a beauty.

'The *rug* is beautiful,' he said, and felt mean watching the sunshine slip from her face.

It was going to be very awkward. The piano, a dark mahogany beast with plenty of brass fittings, looked like it might once have graced the saloon of the Old Bull and Bush. Its music stand was intricately carved in imitation of a more ecclesiastical era. Dear God, he thought as he looked with dismay first at the piano and then a much scribbled-on piece of sheet music for Scott Joplin's *The Entertainer*, in an arrangement that any simpleton should be able to play.

There were many underlinings and bossy pencilled marks: '*Don't forget to lift*' and '*Staccato!*' He could almost picture this Anna's grave face, hair scrunched back and serious grey eyes as she tried to make the jumps, how often she'd have to go back to the beginning to start again; she'd probably curse a bit, get sore shoulders, tendon pains that would shoot from her knuckles to her wrists. She hadn't played as a child. She could bash away for hours but the neural pathways would never really clear. She could 'lift' and 'staccato' to her heart's content but it would never sound right, not even to her untrained ears, he had no doubt about that.

Anna covered the keys with her fingers. She didn't play anything out loud but for a moment it looked as though she could hear the notes in her head. He noticed her earlobe as her hair dropped forward, the neatness of it, and touchingly unpierced.

'I had bad dreams after the removers came,' she said, standing from the piano stool, her fingers still spread out over the keys. 'I had to watch it being taken away because there wasn't school that day. I think my mother got rid of it because she wanted the room for a telly.'

He flipped open the top and forced himself to look into the miserable guts of her piano. He stared at the bar that showed it was over-damped, at the great lump of iron, at the rust and the cobwebs that shouldn't have been there, and then through the broken back panel he saw a dirty great crack in the soundboard.

'All the piano factories that made this sort of English piano went out of business when people got television.' He was stalling, wondering what sort of cruel person would sell her this horrible piano. 'That's why they stopped making them.' She seemed to be waiting for him to say something nice about it, but he knew that however much care he took it was always going to be unstable: this piano was always going to sound crap. It was inside a piano like this one that he once found a dead mouse.

It was straight into wind as he strode away from Evrika Street. His hair whipped his face, making his eyes sting. He was running a passage of the Chopin through his head as the starlings came into view, gathering in dark clouds around the pier. They swooped in formation, plumes and swathes, fluttering like black silk, but no matter how hard he tried, he couldn't make them fit the Barcarolle.

Anna had told him about her recurring dream, she didn't seem to want to hear what he had to say about her piano: she was diving in slow motion through the ocean with the piano slowly spinning away from her; she was trying to reach it. 'My hands shake and my legs are so hopeless and weak that I can't kick myself deeper as the piano sinks into the murk.' She said it was a nightmare, night after night: 'Stuck unable to scream as the falling piano gets smaller and smaller until I can't see it at all.'

She was twisting the neck of her jumper as she spoke: 'It always gives me a really horrible feeling when I wake up', and when she released it, the ribbing was so stretched that it flopped down over her shoulder, revealing a collarbone as shapely as a bow.

He shook his head free of the thought of it. He ought to hurry to the Idlewilds. He pulled his scarf up, covering most of his face as he strode on.

The Idlewilds' Bösendorfer had, apparently, once belonged to a high-ranking SS officer but that off-putting provenance had been hushed up when the piano appeared in England. What on earth had made him think of that? It was Celia Idlewild herself who had once told him but he hadn't given it a thought since. Now, as he drew nearer, he couldn't stop himself from wondering, gloomily, about the SS officer and the Bösendorfer. Goebbels? Mengele? Whose fingerprints stained the ivory keys? His mind grew savage with possibilities: it was from Himmler's secret hideaway outside Salzburg; the Führer himself had taken solace in its silken voice, had worked himself into a frenzy as the Meistersinger Prelude reached its climax like the sound of a hundred crashing trombones heralding the Holocaust.

The waves had got wilder, crashing and folding and throwing stones on to the beach in sequences more fitting to those mighty Wagnerian crescendos than the gentle ripples of his journey to Anna of Evrika Street, when it had seemed as though the sea was playing along with the lilting possibilities of his afternoon.

It was a relief to be inside the Idlewilds' house. All was warmth and calm and fancy cornicing after the punishing wind and waves. He could hear the Bösendorfer already, not badly out of tune as it happened, its shimmering tones and the adagio from Beethoven's Pathétique Sonata getting closer as he followed the neatly packaged figure of Celia Idlewild up the stairs.

Laura Idlewild was seated at the keys. 'Grade seven, next week,' Celia whispered, stopping at the door. Laura hadn't noticed them. She played on.

There it was, the piano of his dreams; wide open and welcoming, its lid curved like a giant wing, the shine of its warm-treacle wood reflecting the chandeliers and inviting him closer.

Laura was at that age where she looked different every time he saw her. She had grown much plumper, not unpleasantly so, and appeared to be wearing a ball gown of blue tulle that had been hacked off mid-thigh. She wasn't playing too incompetently either. He turned away to the big bay windows that faced straight out to sea and as he looked out at the waves smashing on to the shore, the heavy door that led to the balcony started to bang.

Laura stopped playing and Celia sprang across to bolt the balcony door before it banged again. Laura smiled broadly when she spotted him. She was pretty and her eyes were doll-blue but tonight her big gappy-toothed smile made him think of a pumpkin lamp.

'I stopped having the dream as soon as I got this piano,' Anna had told him. Her jumper had stretched and slipped some more and he could see as far as the line the inside of her arm made against her body. Her shoulder gleamed; Richard wanted quite badly to feel the warmth of her skin beneath his fingers and while he stood, not touching, he found that her dream swam into his head as though it were of his own making. The piano falling away through the sea and he was back at the Wigmore Hall, Leszek in the audience with his arm casually draped over Aurelia Lieberman beside him, and his dad, his face pinched and so close that he could see the whites of his eyes and that wet mollusc of his mouth. Richard's hands shaking so badly, and the piano sinking out of his reach, getting smaller and smaller, and with it drowning his dreams.

'I'm very sorry.' He'd never felt meaner, telling poor Anna her piano wasn't worth tuning. He was stepping away from it and wishing he could stop himself from staring at her shoulder. He was appalled to see that he had made her cry, made her offer him a rug, for goodness' sake. She wiped across her eyes quickly with her forearm.

'My poor old Joanna,' she said, attempting to be chirpy. 'The thing is, I wouldn't want to replace it with any other piano.'

'I could help you find something much better.' He had already offered and he offered again more insistently; the thought of driving the Mini with the windows open and her folded into the seat next to him pleased him more than he would ever have thought possible.

He always prided himself on being a very quiet piano tuner, but that night the Bösendorfer took a beating. The notes seemed to resonate through his bones. It was partly to save his own ears that he usually managed to keep the big thumps down to a minimum, really just the one on each key to equalise the strings, but as the wind whipped the rain against the glass, he found himself pounding the keys. His ears were ringing, he was almost punch-drunk by the time he had finished with it. Then, when it was done, his fingers picked up the Chopin and for a moment all was forgiven and he was almost lost, but she came back to find him on the waves of the Barcarolle.

'I don't want another piano. This is *the* piano. It's the one in my dream.' She had followed him down the path in her bare feet.

'It's the same piano. I shipped it here. I had to wait until my aunt died to get it back. She would never let me have it, even though no one played it, and I'm ashamed to say that getting it was the only thing I thought of when she died.' Her eyes were glittering at the memory, but at least she wasn't crying.

'I'm sorry.' He said it again as he shut the front gate.

He had a cold glass of flinty wine in his hand; he'd remained seated at the Idlewilds' piano stool after delightful Celia had suggested he stay and play rather than call a taxi straight away. Graham Idlewild had lit a fire. Celia, who had changed for dinner, perched beside him and their son Ed, a magnificent six feet tall already, sat back to back on the love seat with Laura, her bare legs blushing prettily beneath the shortened dress.

'Chopin's Barcarolle in F Sharp.' He pushed his sleeves to his elbows and flexed his fingers. When he gets it right he can make himself weep.

The Bösendorfer glistened; his fingers hovered above its velvety keys. He lifted his wrists but instead of the Bösendorfer all he could see was Anna's forlorn piano with its nicotined joke of a keyboard. Anna's unpierced earlobe, tender as a new broad bean. Her shoulder. He could hear the stones being flung on to the beach outside. He looked up in panic at the perfection that was the Idlewilds: Graham in his shirtsleeves, wine glass in hand; Celia, so expensively beige; Ed in his school uniform, preternaturally the same age as his father; pretty, plump Laura still smiling at him like a pumpkin. But all he could see was Anna, and the beauty of the rug that she made from rags. The Bösendorfer was sinking fast, as though through the colours of her rug, a setting sun, a stormy sea, and his hands began to shake.

The Man Across
the River

'Fear grips me from behind, with a knife to my throat. Fear wears a dark cloak. He mourns the loss of his wife. He's on drugs. . .'

My mother laughs a little cruelly as she reads from the stapled sugar-paper book. It's a childhood dirge, yes, one of mine that she's just found in an old biscuit tin.

'They were always so full of terror.' She chuckles, turning the page with an air of confusion, and I try to raise my eyebrows at Simon in a *See what I have to put up with?* sort of a way without her noticing.

She has taken to wearing kaftans of Demis Roussos proportions of late and her hair hangs down her back in a single long grey plait: a bell-pull that secretly I long to tug. I silently thank Simon for ignoring Tim, his twin brother, when he advised him to take a long hard look at the mother before considering the daughter as a wife.

She reaches into the Peak Freans tin and unfolds another

effort, clears her throat, ready to mock. It's about a dead jackdaw.

'What do you think of Mummy's poem?' she asks when the jackdaw is duly buried, possibly still alive, in the cruel black earth of my childhood imagination, but Angus and Ivan are more interested in picking the combination lock on her sweets and treasures box than listening to any poem.

'Do you know Mummy won a prize?'

'I had my name in the newspaper,' I tell the boys, who look at me blankly.

'It was for the poem that you wrote about cruise missiles,' my mother remembers. Simon snorts loudly into his mug of tea and she gives him that teacher's look of hers, only these days it rarely works as a corrective, it's just funny.

'Do you think the boys want to watch Cee-bee-bees?' she asks, clapping her hands together, and I almost grind my teeth as the boys jump down, crying: 'Cee-bee-bees! Cee-bee-bees!'

'It's really quite educational.' She leads them off, plait swinging, and as usual I wonder if she's playing an elaborate game.

'It's ridiculous,' I moan to Simon. 'I was never allowed to watch television.' Now she seems to revel in turning my children into couch potatoes. She even bought a DVD of an American television show purporting to be child-friendly science that, when they all watched it, turned out to be nothing but overgrown boys demonstrating massive ejaculations using the explosive properties of Mentos and Diet Cola. Bombs and sweets and America, all at the flick of a switch. What fun. And she buys them sweeties, or even *candy*, to cram into their mouths while they watch this stuff, though she draws the line at Haribo, which she tells them are made from boiled-down bones and will give them cancer. Then she has to explain to them about cancer.

'What sort of child writes poems about cruise missiles?' Simon asks, picking it out of the tin and holding it up. There's an illustration of a wire fence with a rabbit hanging from it, done in felt-tips, and I'm surprised to see how my writing used to slope backwards as though my letters were all trying to jam on the brakes.

Simon goes to her pantry for a loaf of bread so that we can all have toast. White sliced bread, I notice.

'Funnily enough,' I say, 'I can remember writing it.'

It had been fine and dusty that day, the ground hard beneath my flip-flops, the grass just beginning to get scorched, bright sun I could feel against my skin. I was pleased with my tan, I liked the tickle of the grass on my bare brown arms and legs and I had a small white dog at my heels, a rather bouncy and optimistic terrier that my mother had taken pity on.

Up at the cottage she was busy plotting the next revolution with her friend Suzanne. Their uniform was pretty standard dangly earrings and CND T-shirts, their brigade the militant wing of Primary School Teachers for Peace, against Coca-Cola, fur coats, fighting, whatever.

Suzanne had been my class teacher, as well as being my mother's first lieutenant and partner in placards, and was still in the habit of demanding that I write poetry. In those days I couldn't ask her to pass the salt without her thinking I should write about passing salt, though it was usually current affairs that my self-appointed muse felt should inspire

49

me: starving Africans, homelessness, the sort of things that eleven-year-old girls are keen not to think about too much.

'You should write a poem about the cruise missiles,' she said to me that sunny afternoon. 'It would be interesting to have a child's-eye view of the danger.'

She and my mother had already scared me witless with stories of nuclear attack: it was all coming to Britain, they said, while gloomily sipping their rosehip tea. 'Bloody Americans again.'

Suzanne and my mother were considering going to Greenham Common for the holidays. 'We have to do our bit to stop them storing their missiles here,' they said. 'Sitting ducks we'll be. We have to go for the sake of our children', and they looked at me cramming my mouth with peanut butter from a spoon and nodded.

I had seen Greenham Common on the news: the high fences and the righteous feral women, in the mud, arms linked, singing protest songs and shouting: 'Whose side are you on?' at the dead-eyed troops.

'I don't think I could live with myself another moment if I didn't do my bit to keep the missiles out.' My mother was emphatic and I didn't think I could live for another moment full stop if I had to stay and listen to another word. I slipped from my chair and headed for the door.

'It might be fun to live in a bender, take the kids,' Suzanne was saying and I thought how much more fun it would be if they all dropped dead. Suzanne's own children were much younger than me. One of each, with perma-nently encrusted nostrils. They looked like trolls with their fuzzy hair and the girl, whose name was Coriander, had a habit of following me around.

I knew from a home-educated girl with a lisp at Woodcraft Folk that a bender was an unglamorous tent made out of bent-over saplings and tarpaulin. She had already been to Greenham Common and the news from the front wasn't good: lavatories that were holes in the ground, 'everyone stinks like wet dogs'. I wondered why I couldn't just spend the summer on a beach somewhere with my dad.

I rolled up my vest in the way that my mother hated me to do and trudged along for a bit on the dirt track past the hazel woods, whipping the heads from weeds and long grass with a swishy branch I'd pulled from a sapling. The white terrier was doing its best to lighten me up, springing back and forth, bringing me the black corpse of a tennis ball that it'd found in the long grass.

Cruise was such a wind-in-the-hair carefree word, I thought, whipping the dry grass, sending little darts of grass-seed flying. Cruise. I choose. To amuse. There were rusty-brown butterflies at every footfall and birds singing, an endless sky that matched the faded denim of my cut-offs. I threw the ball and the dog jumped for it. I swung my arms, enjoying their length and slenderness and the near-burn of the sun on my shoulders.

Heading towards the river I decided that cruise missiles were probably bad in the way that sweets were bad for the teeth, and television, particularly American television, was bad for the soul.

I knew these fields well from walking with my mother. The farmer would be topping the grass for hay soon so I should try not to make tracks and opted for the well-trodden path along the riverbank. Until all this stuff about

Greenham Common had arisen the long summer had stretched before me as blissfully as empty golden sands. I was dying for school to end. There were girls in the third form with spiteful nails. In the loos there were girls who waited for you to thump you, to write your name on the wall, to surround you and bruise you or nuke you with their words. Sign here if you hate so and so.

Cruise. The last thing I needed was another thing to be afraid of. The terrier ran for the ball and startled a duck who shot from the reeds, desperately calling to her ducklings who fell in two by two behind her, leaving chevrons in their wake.

Cruise, cruising by. The river was at its widest, practically a pool and smooth as glass. In the winter it flooded completely and the footpath was submerged in knee-deep water meadow, it even had a current running through it then. In the spring the drowned grass was flattened and feathered, littered with plastic bottles. But in the summer the grass was tall and unswayed with buttercups, and lily pads bloomed on the black river that ran through it, easing itself along the sloping bank from which some people swam, though not me because I never liked the ooze of mud between my toes.

I stopped for a moment on the bank and watched the river slip by, its glossy surface shirred by the breeze and stippled with small circles from darting insects. A pair of damselflies were disco dancers, dressed in blue sequins. The water lily buds looked fit to burst their corsets in the heat.

The bank on the opposite side of the river was in shadow and heavily wooded so I didn't see him at first. A couple of times as I wandered along the sunny side I thought I saw a flash of white in the woods and I later realised that this must have been the white of his T-shirt.

I could only look once. First, I saw his dogs snuffling around and then the man emerged between the trees. The dogs were large, not a breed I recognised, with muscular hind limbs and hacksawed tails. The man was powerfully built too, his white T-shirt looked stretched across his chest and he was holding a stick. His hair stuck up from his head, an army sort of style, so blond it was almost yellow. He didn't look like the sort of person that you normally encountered on a footpath and I was immediately glad that we had a river between us. It was the stick in his hand that spooked me most: it wasn't long and thin like a walking stick, nor was it the sort of rough stick that you might throw for a dog. His stick was squat and thick at the end like a baseball bat and he was holding it in front of his chest like he meant business.

I found myself walking a bit faster and calling to the little terrier, though I wasn't quite sure which way to head. Jumping beans had started in my stomach. I kept walking faster still and wondered if I was crazy to have this reaction to a man out walking his dogs. The spit in my mouth turned to paste as I tried to work out how far I was from the bridge that separated his side of the river from mine. I rounded the bend and the bleached carcass of the lightning oak came into view. The oak, I knew, wasn't far beyond the bridge; if I could see the bleached oak then the iron bridge that crossed the river was maybe five minutes away at a fast pace. I'd frightened myself enough by then to turn heel and started heading back in the direction I'd come, trying not to run at first. When I

did run I felt foolish, almost cursing myself, my disbe-
lieving legs disobeying me all the way.

They seemed to have taken on a life of their own: it was
as though at each step my ankles and knees had become
spongy, cartilage rather than bone. I tripped on a rut, my
ankle twisted, and it was as I clambered back up on to my
knees that I knew for sure that the man had indeed turned
around and was keeping up because I could see his dogs
reflected in the river.

I pounded along, not even aware of the pain in my
ankle; I saw the dogs running, heard the crack of branches
from across the water. Though we had left the lightning
oak bridge far behind I knew there was another bridge, a
stone one, just ahead. I was going to have to veer off the
path and cut across the fields to get back to the cottage
quickly; it would only be trespassing a little bit. It seems
mad now that my degree of trespass should even have
entered my mind. I might have done better to think about
the barbed wire fences and hedges I would have to fight my
way through. As I started to run up the field I heard a splash
and turned to look back at the river. The two dogs were
crouched over the bank, barking. The man's head appeared,
breaking the surface like a seal; the sunlight hit the rivulets
running off his shoulders as his arms parted the river around
him in a muscular vee. He was shouting to me but I couldn't
hear what as my heart hammered in my ears. It just sounded
like, 'Oi oi oi.'

Fear gripped me. I ripped my thigh on the barbed wire
of the first fence. I raced on, barely aware of the blood running down the inside of my leg and having to rid myself of
my flip-flops which were getting tangled between the toes

with grass, as if trying to run wasn't hard enough anyway. I fell over twice, expecting to see the man looming over me as I scrambled to my feet. I could hear his dogs bark and as I hurtled past the hazel copse I almost imagined I could see the shadow of his club, their breath at my heels.

I didn't go back to the river all summer long. It was restful to be in the company of the women and the girls at the camp, gathering firewood on the Common, singing songs, becoming gently smoked by the fire. I became skilled at fence rattling and chanting: 'Take the toys from the boys!' I wore tie-dye and rainbow braids in my hair. I enjoyed the singing but grew to hate the underwater sounds of the ululating at the fence.

We ate loads of apples and cheese instead of meals and I pretended not to mind when someone shouted 'Lesbians!' out of the car window while my mother and I were walking up the hot tarmac to find a standpipe.

When we packed up our stuff at the end of the summer I tied my floppy stuffed rabbit to the perimeter fence. The part of the fence where we camped was festooned with other people's toys and bras and babies' booties and bits and pieces that were supposed to remind everyone of peace. Suzanne's children tied their teddy bears to it. My mother handed me a shoelace and I fixed the small silky-eared rabbit to a higher part of the fence where it immediately hung its head like any other tatty thing. It seemed a pity then because I had slept with my nose pressed to its silky ears for every night I could remember.

I never told my mother about the man across the river because I couldn't be sure about what I had seen. It only happened a couple of weeks before we left for Greenham

Common and my shame had grown by the day. I was first to switch on the local news every night and I scoured the county gazette. After a while I doubted myself more and more and the face of a drowning man started to surface in my dreams and I would wake with the sheets wound around my legs like weeds. When we moved later that year, though I had loved the cottage and my bedroom in the eaves, I was relieved that I would never have to go anywhere near the river again.

Simon puts the cruise missiles poem down. 'You poor little thing,' he says, ruffling my hair, and I nearly cry. From the other room we can hear the blare of Cee-bee-bees and Angus's throaty laugh. 'Daddy,' he calls.

I refold the poem and fix the lid back on the tin.

'Your mother wants to know if we're bringing the kids to the climate change demo on Sunday.' Simon's her messenger, returning to the kitchen with an article she's clipped from the *Guardian*. 'She said she thought we ought to.'

'Did you tell her that last week Angus had nightmares every night about the sun exploding?' I say.

Unlike my mother, I don't want Angus and Ivan to have to worry about cancer or have images of people jumping from burning tower blocks scorched into their retinas. I don't want the terror to live in the marrow of my children's growing bones.

Simon shrugs. 'It's climate change,' he says. 'It's all about them—'

I interrupt. 'They don't like crowds,' I say, and gesturing with my thumb towards the noise of canned laughter: 'And I'm not like her.'

Simon shushes me.

'Remember when Angus was a baby and we took him to the Iraq War demonstration in Hyde Park?' My mother has come back into the kitchen though she'd kicked her shoes off in the other room and I didn't hear her approach. 'You and Simon didn't dress properly,' she says.

'What?' I say.

'You were both freezing.' She says it as though somehow even in protesting we were deficient and I wonder if she overheard me telling Simon that I was different from her, telling him as though being different from her was something to boast about.

Remembering the demonstration makes me shiver. As it happens my clothing had been perfectly adequate against the clear cold day, as was Simon's: thick padded jackets, pashminas and hats. My mother worried that people taking photographs were from MI5. 'Look at that man,' she kept saying when we'd finally come to a standstill with the crowds in the park. 'Dressed in tawny colours, big camera. He's not part of the protest. He's here to keep a record of the people.'

'Don't be so paranoid,' I said, laughing.

'Look, he's systematically moving along the lines. He doesn't look right.'

There were two million people in Hyde Park that day and not a single arrest. Having Angus in his pushchair made me feel historic, like Demeter charged with a flaming torch. It was his future we were all shouting about, my fists were aloft with the rest of them. Ken Livingstone called for peace, and I looked at Angus sleeping, wrapped safe and warm in his cocoon, just his palely beautiful face appearing from the folds like a Russian doll.

My mother was carrying a banner that said NOT IN MY NAME, and wearing a colourful Peruvian knitted hat with little woollen plaits that made her look like a rather incongruous schoolgirl. She met a woman in the crowd and they embraced. 'Yes, here we are again,' she said, shaking her woolly plaits. 'Nothing changes.'

It was during a lull in the speeches that she told me what she'd read in that morning's newspaper. Something grisly about a missing girl and a man who drove a butcher's van.

'Remember the one?' she asked. I shook my head. 'It was a green van. When we lived at Riversdale,' she prompted, raising her arm in a fist as high as her shoulder would allow her. 'Impeach Bush, Impeach Blair!'

'I thought you were vegetarians,' Simon said, blowing into his hands and putting them back into his pockets.

'We were vegetarians,' said my mother, as wistfully as a woman remembering her miniskirt days, 'but it didn't stop him calling. No matter how often I told him we didn't eat meat, he still called in the van every Friday.

'Impeach Bush, Impeach Blair! It *stank* of meat,' she said. 'Sometimes, I think, he hunted deer with his dogs, and butchered them himself. Oh, what a horrible thought. It's been in all the newspapers, you know.'

Something small but monstrous was hatching in my memory.

'That's what the smell was,' she said, 'the venison. In the end I had to ring up the butcher and complain but I think he still came even after that.'

I thought I could picture the green van parked outside our cottage, the blond man hulked at the wheel. The thing that was hatching grew tentacles that slithered down the back of my neck.

'It's horrible to think of myself talking to him now,' she continued.

There was something glinting in my mother's eyes that made me think of a cat bringing a mouse to the door. 'It must have been around the same time that he did it,' she said, shuddering. 'Around the time he used to park outside our place. They only caught him because of his DNA on a completely separate charge.'

Just then Angus started to whimper. My breast tingled, filling with milk. It was as though it was a separate entity, beating to a different tune, with a different conductor from the other parts of my body. A man from the United Nations had just taken to the podium and a cheer went up from the crowd. The rest of me was running with ice but my only thought was that I would have to find a bench to sit down and produce warm milk to comfort my crying son.

Leaving Hamburg

Aurelia Lieberman didn't give a damn what the driver thought. 'Slow down!' she shouted and grabbed at her seatbelt, tugging hard at the inertia reel, too hard to be effective. The wheels of the taxi spun a little as the driver took pole position at the lights and a red rose flew from the seat so she had to strike out a hand to stop it being thrown to the floor.

Langsam! she almost snapped at him, hoping the word applied to the speed of a car as it did to music.

Snow was piled deeply by the kerbs, it wasn't the time to be playing Michael Schumacher. It was still snowing lightly, though thankfully the roads had been efficiently gritted. She tugged again at the seatbelt, another sullen clonk.

What was it about this wretched driver that was making her so pissed off? Normally she would be careful to hide her nerves beneath a veneer of good manners. She'd endeavour to fasten her seatbelt sneakily, quietly, minding too much about a leather-gloved ego. She was the same with waiters: it was impossible to send back corked wine or point out when a bill had been wrongly added up. The bouquets she received in her dressing room after a piano recital were always deemed by her to be lovely, really lovely, even the ones that contained lilies or tuberoses to which she was allergic. She had never once in her life, as far as she could remember, taken anything back to a shop.

With the seatbelt clipped, at last, firmly into place, Aurelia briefly checked the plane ticket in her wallet; out of habit she extracted a slightly dog-eared picture of her only child, Claudine. Looking at her daughter did nothing to improve her mood. This elfin child was years out of date but she didn't feel exactly impelled to replace it with the current mouthy version: a Claudine who had confessed only last week to a tattoo; a garish butterfly inked for ever on to her previously lovely ankle. Aurelia leaned her forehead against the cool glass of the window and settled her gaze on a Hamburg cloaked by the snow.

Claudine's tattoo: a single splash of graffiti, no longer a guilty secret; a lone dark dog shit scrawled on the snow-covered pavement.

The hiss of the snow against the tyres gave her a chill. She should have thought to bring a proper coat. The first flurries arrived last night while she was being so courteously delivered from her hotel to the concert hall, a better driver than this one and a smarter car – wasn't that always the way *before* the concert – and Hamburg still just any city, then.

Dressed in her finery: the full-length black velvet that she favoured for performance, eyes closed, hands in a knot. A modest jewel at her breast: Ann Boleyn on her way to the

Tower. Blood rushing, nerves thrumming, except only in the usual pre-concert way, not like she was about to lose her head. She was not under-rehearsed, she knew that. And Brahms had always been kind. By the time she opened her eyes she was surprised to see the snow swirling all around like freshly plucked goose feathers, enough for the chauffeur to switch the wipers to full.

The pillow fight must have lasted all night and still no sign of an armistice, as bursts of snow whirled and tumbled around streets of solemn houses lying beneath pristine eiderdowns.

Tucking the angelic Claudine back into her wallet with a sigh, Aurelia remembered a time, before airport security became such killjoys, when, from a trip just like this, she had filled a cool bag with Alpine snow and taken it home for Claudine. There had been enough for a small snowman and a couple of snowballs and Claudine's serious little face had been pure sunshine.

'Your first time in Hamburg?' The taxi driver interrupted her thoughts. His English was better than his driving.

Aurelia nodded. 'But my father's family . . .' She trailed off, hoping he'd ask her no more and concentrate instead on the road in front, where a tall coach was scattering blinding white flurries in its wake.

Aurelia wiped condensation from the window with her sleeve. All along the pavements the snow was unsullied. Not even a snowman in sight. In the gardens the trees and shrubs had been silenced by it, expertly iced, even the sleeping cars looked festive so she could almost believe it was pretty.

She checked her watch. Still early for snowmen. She

reminded herself to leave enough time to stop at the Duty Free for a bottle of pong requested by Claudine, something called 'Destiny', or was it 'Dynasty'? She settled back and let her fingers play at the familiar round pip of her grandmother's moonstone, fastened to the grey scarf at her neck.

Bobo's moonstone had passed to Aurelia at a time when the death of her grandmother was enough to send her so deep into the black hole that she thought she might never climb out. The bad news came at the same time as her break-up with Leszek Smolsky. Leszek, the possessor of the most beautiful fingers she had ever seen on a keyboard: long and pale and fluent as hands are in a dream of water. Leszek: young, Polish, a pianist who would break anyone's heart just by playing.

Her grandmother's death was a very dark darkness, even before Leszek's decision. She was already down when he kicked her.

Aurelia had never managed to imagine a life without Bobo. She grew up with the delicate weight of her grandmother's dreams draped around her shoulders like a well-chosen shawl. She played most expressively when Bobo was in the audience. And it wasn't only music: when Aurelia was a reluctant reader at seven or eight, books with exciting heroines would arrive in return for short reviews. Where the brightly painted school craft things that Aurelia occasionally presented to her father went largely unnoticed, her artistic endeavours, however cack-handed – blobby flowerpots, papier mâché fish and the like – were received by Bobo with more joy than anything anyone could have bought from a shop. She was an exceptional pen pal, often including bars of Lindt or marzipan with her letters. She sent sheet music from Chappell's. She liked to know that Aurelia had a clean face flannel and made chocolate mousse from whipped cream and grated chocolate and jumping jacks from cardboard and thread. Bobo paid for all the music lessons, though it was a mystery how she managed it.

Aurelia's father brought her Bobo's moonstone with an inadequate hug in the late morning of that dismal November day. Leszek arrived empty-handed in the evening. One look at Leszek with his arms hanging by his sides told her everything: it seemed pointless to mention her grandmother. No, there wasn't anyone else, he assured her. He'd decided to go while there was still time for her to meet someone else. If she should want children, she'd need time. His decency rankled, even now.

She remembered how he did it: in a letter that she'd refused to read that he'd propped on the music stand of her piano, tears inking his already ludicrously dense lashes. Leszek's eyelashes would always make every woman he met think about having his baby. That and the way he played Chopin, long strong fingers playing the keys so softly they might have been stroking the cheek of an infant.

She couldn't look at him when he came back for his things: his camera, his books, his leather music case, his black cashmere jumpers; not many things but everything so right. An old-fashioned camera, the jumpers folded neatly one on top of the other, shaving cream that smelled cruelly of lilacs, an apologetic smile.

So there she was with Leszek in the doorway, too handsome to look at; dishevelled and still in her nightie, talking to a mouse that had appeared from behind the piano: 'Oh, Bobo, what am I going to do?'

And maybe because he realised that her grandmother had died, he had taken pity on her one last time, or maybe it was simply because the rain hammered the windows and he didn't feel like getting wet. It rained like that all through the night and though it was punctuated by shuddering sobs, it had been the sweetest that Aurelia had ever known.

The traffic had slowed and the driver drummed his leather fingers on the steering wheel before switching on the radio. Synthesizer pop jangled her ears.

Bobo's moonstone was a typically modest jewel set in a plain gold bar, silky beneath the tip of her thumb. Bobo had worn it pinned to a scarf or on the lapel of one of the suits of fine grey and blue wool that had lasted her a lifetime. She had style, was clever with a needle, invisible mending, mothballs. Her ground-floor flat had bright red chairs and proper linen at the table, a bit elegant for the brick-built block in Muswell Hill, where the rowan berries made a mess on the pavements in the autumn, and rowdy children snogged and jeered and drank cheap cider outside her bedroom window all year round.

The driver turned off the main Grindelallee and into wide streets that were more Belgravia than Muswell Hill. Creamy, cold imperious houses presided and no one about to enjoy the snow. Aurelia found herself scanning the powdered facades: a colonnaded porch here, an ornate balcony there, a cupola fringed with snow.

Bobo had shown her a drawing once, on a much-folded and refolded sheet of green writing paper, of the house in Hamburg. It was a house of pleasing symmetery, with bay windows and a wisteria climbing to the third floor. There had been, Bobo recalled, a plaster centaur above the front door. 'Always such a cheerful creature to pass on the way in.'

The snow was thickly padded all the way up the edges of the Mittelweg, for as far as the eye could see. The driver seemed to have slowed down, as though out of respect for the houses they passed, and Aurelia couldn't help looking for the centaur above every door. She imagined Bobo setting off along this very pavement: a determined young woman, coiled dark plait pinned at her nape, woollen coat and laced-up leather snow boots, flanked by two shyly smiling boys, each with a hand in hers, and bending forwards from the waist, telling them not to slip.

Aurelia remembered the squeeze of that hand. Her grandmother's voice, she never lost the accent, of course: 'Give me *deine kleine* paw to keep you safe, *mein Baerchen*.'

Their boots would have made the only footprints.

Second-hand memories were blowing about the Hamburg streets like litter. Kristallnacht. In the morning Bobo told her two little boys to look at how prettily the glass glittered on the pavements to stop them feeling so frightened. She never once let them see her cry.

Aurelia felt the heat rise from the pit of her stomach, last night's embers, the red rose blazing.

'*Bitte . . .*' She leaned forward to the taxi driver and said in her faltering German: '*Zur Jüdischen . . .*' and then she couldn't remember the word and had to fumble for her phrase book.

'*Friedhof,*' he said, before she had found the word 'cemetery', and with a rather exaggerated performance of the U-turn that this entailed, he agreed to take her there. She held the rose on her lap and tried not to become engulfed by thoughts of last night's audience and the panic attack that had left her speechless and graceless standing before them.

It happened as the rose was thrown on to the stage at the end of her performance, while she was standing from the piano offering a silent prayer of thanks to Brahms and to the grandfather she had never met. The audience clapping, and the rose arriving in an arc from several rows back, landing at her feet, long-stemmed and glamorous. As she bent to pick it up, suddenly she could hear Bobo's voice. The blood rushing in her ears. At first just a whisper: 'They smashed his violin', and Aurelia, taking her bow, eyes lowered, found that she couldn't bring herself to look up at a single face of the audience.

'I was glad he was already dead and didn't have to witness it.' There was a pulse of her heart, a bitter taste in her mouth and in her ears more insistent this time: 'They smashed his violin.' Who smashed his violin? Roaring in her ears. The audience cheering as one, but still her eyes were fixed to the polished wooden boards. She thought of Bobo in Muswell Hill. She didn't think she could move. Bobo pouring coffee from a tall bone-china pot, telling her about Georg who could make an audience weep, so exquisite was his feel for the strings of his violin. Someone whooped. She was still too afraid to look up. Her grandfather probably played this very hall. Who smashed his violin? Without a word, she picked up the rose that was lying at her feet and fled.

Who smashed his violin? When Bobo told her stories, Aurelia hadn't always paid as much attention as she now wished she had; it seemed there had always been something else on her mind.

Whenever Aurelia took a plane she thought of Bobo. Bobo was nervous when her loved ones had to fly. She impressed on Aurelia that survivors were generally the people with a plan: they paid attention to the safety demonstration, she said, and counted the seats to the nearest emergency exit; they kept their shoes on their feet in case they needed to escape over jagged surfaces and took care to dress in natural fibres that wouldn't melt and burn their faces off.

Aurelia stashed the Duty Free bag containing Claudine's perfume into the overhead locker and briefly nodded to the man in the window seat. He looked pleasant enough. She took a small Valium as she settled into her own seat beside him, kicking off her shoes and ignoring the air hostess who was gently choreographing a really quite boring disaster at the front. She touched the moonstone pin and offered a prayer to anyone who cared to listen.

In the Jewish cemetery Aurelia's red rose now lay on a thick pillow of snow. Her grandfather's grave had a number. Bobo had once written it down for her. In case she should ever go to Hamburg, she said. 'No reason why you should.'

The iron gates to the Jewish cemetery had been locked. Aurelia had waded through the snow, which was up to her knees, but the spiked bars of the fence were too high for her to climb.

She considered attaching a piece of paper with the number of the grave, and her grandfather's name, to the stem of the rose but in the end she simply threw it over the fence. It would be a rare bloom: there wouldn't be many in there to go round. She remembered Bobo once saying that it was a miracle that the graves had survived, especially

Georg's, having been so late on. The last she'd seen of it, just before she left Hamburg, it was still bare earth. As Bobo left the cemetery that final time she was jeered at.

Bobo had been almost eighty when she broke her arm running down the hill for a bus to the Opera House. Aurelia could picture her afterwards in that plain white flat in Muswell Hill with her arm in plaster. Calling herself a fool. Upright high-backed armchair. Passing a magnifying glass with a mother-of-pearl handle over the *Guardian* crossword. A bun and pearly combs as translucent as the hair they held, the tender pink glow of her scalp and her head moving over the paper like the moon over water.

A small glass of Dubonnet by her side. 'Ach, try not to worry about me', taking a tiny sip, while the swearing and spitting reached its peak outside in the dark.

Her smile to Aurelia was sweet and wistful, almost far-away, or maybe she was still thinking about the crossword clue. 'I have nothing to steal.' She put down the magnifying glass and patted the moonstone pinned to her silk scarf. 'Apart, *meine kleine sonne*, from this . . .'

The moonstone drew light from the lamp. 'Your parents bought this so that I would have something to leave you.' The lovely milk lustre within the smooth cabochon gleamed as she moved, the same blue adularescence as her failing eyes. Aurelia could see the slight curve of her widow's hump.

'*Kleine sonne*.' How lovely it had been to be her grandmother's little sun.

The only newspaper on the flight was in German. Aurelia took one anyway and stared at the front-page picture of an old man and a younger woman stepping out of a limousine beneath a headline: RAUB VON BILLIONAR'S

SARG. The woman was an upswept blonde in royal-blue satin and jewels, a fixed smile that made Aurelia think of a leopard she'd once seen pacing the bars at the Berlin Zoo. Around her neck a collar of pearls the size of eyeballs. Beside her the grey-haired man didn't look quite so pleased to be having his picture taken, pale lips tightly pressed together like strips of Velcro.

The German man in the window seat beside her leaned over and pointed to the story.

'Stolen from his mausoleum in the middle of the night,' he said. He spoke perfect English, despite his accent, and had thick cropped hair in various shades of grey that leapt from his crown in a single whirl like a Viennese Fancy.

'How awful,' said Aurelia. The man had good clean hands, with square-ended fingertips. 'Why would anyone do that?'

'His father funded the Nazis. That's how the family got so rich.'

He prodded the photograph of the couple, so resplendent on their night out. 'Maybe his coffin was full of gold,' he said. 'Like a pharaoh.'

An air hostess bustled by to collect half-drunk cups of complimentary orange juice, checking that seatbelts had been fastened, suspicious as a store detective: 'Could you lift your cardigan so that I can check your belt, please, madam?' – which made the man in the window seat snort, and when Aurelia looked up she saw that his smile made the corners of his eyes crinkle like a cat's whiskers. 'They always refused to pay reparation, someone has probably taken him as a protest,' he said.

'Good,' Aurelia replied, folding the couple in on themselves and stuffing the newspaper into the seat pocket in front of her. 'I hope they never give the body back', and as the blood rushed to her cheeks she wondered why the Valium hadn't taken effect.

She took Claudine's photograph from her wallet and immediately regretted that it made her think about that vile tattoo, stuck for ever, like a big blot on her ankle. She settled the badly shaped cushion into the small of her back. Some stains never wash out. She thought of Bobo's upstairs neighbour Bela with her eyes always hidden behind large dark glasses, even at night, and a number inked to her wrist: that number was all you could think about when you met her, even when she was wearing long sleeves and gloves. The man next to her had returned unperturbed to looking out of his window at the fading light. The plane rumbled along the runway and she wondered if she had left it too late to take another half-Valium.

They were accelerating and she could feel every jolt. Everything rattling. She wished she hadn't called Claudine such a horrible name before she left. Stains that don't wash out, scars that never fade. She thought about Bobo waving her sons off on the train, labels around their necks, trying her best to appear jaunty. An adventure! Leaving Hamburg. What a long five months it must have been between the Kindertransport and her own passage out.

As the plane took off Aurelia realised what a fool she'd been to have never got around to making her will. It was the same as not watching the safety demonstration: an inability to think about the unthinkable. She regretted that she'd never tried to contact Leszek, despite the passing of the years. She regretted that she would die intestate.

As they roared into the sky, she thought of the jewellery box on her dressing table at home and Claudine like a little magpie as a child, raiding it and running around the house, sparkling and jingling. Lovely little voice, a song from school assemblies: 'Sing Hosanna! Sing Hosanna!'

These days Claudine wore thick silver rings, even one on her thumb, and lots of bracelets, metal ones and grubby ones made from string. Aurelia couldn't imagine Claudine with any of her jewellery: not her ruby earrings, nor her lapis lazuli beads. Claudine would never know that it had been Leszek who had given Aurelia the amber bracelet that she wore for good luck every birthday. She wouldn't know the significance of the moonstone either, wouldn't know about Bobo because Aurelia had failed to write an addendum of wishes, and would probably lose it or swap it with a friend for tickets to a band. Bobo's simple brooch wouldn't fit with the ripped jeans and racy underwear. There was a new cranking noise as the plane gathered height. She'd left it too late to read the safety instructions. It sounded like teeth and hammers. Aurelia gripped her head in her hands.

'It's just the undercarriage coming up,' the German man explained. 'Try not to worry.' And she wished that he would hold her hand.

As they reached altitude, the noise subsided. The German man patted her arm and asked in his good English if she would join him in a glass of wine and, wiping her eyes, Aurelia agreed.

She sipped her wine and the fist around her heart loosened its grip. Aurelia could see her daughter, quite clearly, in the future, but not too soon: she'd be wearing a black beret, a macintosh tied at her waist with a wide belt. The beret would be just right, pulled down jauntily over one side of her face, leaving one eye peeping out through the unmistakably extravagant lashes that Claudine had inherited from her father. Aurelia's eyes were watering again: airplanes often made her tearful. She wiped them with her fingertips, brushing everything away. Claudine with the moonstone pinned to her beret: the girl had style, and she found herself turning to the man beside her and clinking her glass to his.

The Birthday Present

It wasn't a great start to his birthday: me in my shabby dressing gown, hair a bit frazzly, in need of a cut. 'I didn't get you a present.'

He looked at me, blinking, a little myopic without his glasses, as though I might be a magician about to release a flock of doves from my sleeve.

'Really, I didn't . . .'

His soft brown eyes suddenly downcast. He looked away but I'd already seen the boy in him. For a moment I thought he might cry. I glanced quickly to where the real boys were making birthday cards with the bits of paper I'd hastily folded in half.

'I couldn't think of the right thing,' I lied, unable to tell him the truth. 'I'm sorry.' There was really nothing else I could say: I wasn't ill and as far as he knew there was money in my account. I was twisting my wedding ring around my finger just to give myself something to look at. The truth was I'd forgotten to give his birthday any thought at all.

'It's OK, I think I'll survive.' He laughed then, even planted a kiss on my unworthy cheek, while Ivan and Angus, up on stools, kicked the cupboards, coloured pencils in their fists.

Simon rinsed his coffee mug at the sink, using his thumb to remove the ring from last night's last cup. As a consequence of that last cup he was probably awake for hours after I'd flaked out. He usually is.

Simon ruffled my hair with both hands, vigorously, in the way that a rugby player might express kinship after a try.

'I told you, it doesn't matter at all,' he said, and the slight flush in his cheeks made him look ridiculously healthy, like the sort of person who might run a marathon. It suited him living out here.

I took the coffee cup from him and wished I didn't feel quite so like the bad fairy at the feast. Simon deserved better. If only the postman would come there'd be cards from other people, a parcel from his mother. But the postman always comes so late; it's not like London around here. I made Simon his coffee and frothed up the milk a little so it looked like a cappuccino. At least it was a beautiful morning. A golden light from the garden poured over the table, yesterday's buttercups glimmered in their jar. Simon sat down and rested his head on his forearms in front of him and I put the coffee down and hugged him because I really did feel sorry, and laid my cheek across the back of his nubbly jumper.

Ivan slid on to his knee and held his paper card to his face, too close for him to focus.

'It's you in a space rocket, Daddy,' he said.

Nearly every one of Ivan's pictures is of one of these rather phallic space rockets. On the occasion of his birthday, Ivan had drawn Simon with lots of curly grey hair, which was a little unfair because he still has plenty of brown, and glasses. The effect was rather elderly for an astronaut but the rocket was magnificent. Simon snorted. Angus laid his card on top of his brother's, everything always a fratricidal fight to the death: 'Thirty-seven candles, Daddy. Count them', and Simon did his best to look equally pleased with both of his sons' drawings.

He and the boys started splashing milk on to their cereal. I was feeling restless already, buttering my toast and trying not to think about you. I was testing myself to see if today might be the day that I would find the will power not to run to you as soon as the coast was clear. Simon sipped his coffee and picked up a yellow and green polythene wallet of Snappy Snaps from the table where I'd left it. He started flicking through, unhurried, though I was sure he ought to get going. Usually, I tried not to leave photos lying around but as this lot was mostly of Ivan I hadn't bothered to hide them.

'Some of these are quite good,' he said, swilling his mouth like a man tasting wine, and I felt myself blush.

He took another leisurely sip from his mug as he reached the last photograph; this was one that I'd allowed Ivan to snap of me. Rather harried by the window.

'It was only fair to let him have a go after he'd agreed to look so lovingly at the flowers,' I explained.

Simon was tapping Ivan's snap before him like a playing card.

'Now, this I like,' he said.

I couldn't imagine why he would. I was wearing a polo neck that looked almost fuzzy, it was so pilled, and jeans and old plimsolls with my knees bent up and legs akimbo along the arm of the chair to fit into Ivan's shot. I didn't look especially comfortable and my hair was a mess.

'Though, I'd like it even more,' he said, quite poker-faced, '. . . without clothes on.'

'Shhhh.' I glanced from Simon to the boys, who were busy flicking crumbs at each other, and wondered if I'd heard him right.

'Come on, chaps, get your blazers,' he said, and left for the car with the boys tugging his hands like fairground balloons on the end of their strings.

I knew, as soon as he'd driven off, that I should get myself into town and sort out a present: better late than never and, as I've said, Simon deserved better.

I started hunting for my car keys. I used to keep them on the peg by the back door but recently I've started to throw them down in the strangest places. I half hoped that I wouldn't find them, and then I'd be able to spend another day with you, just the two of us; worry about Simon's present who knew when. At the very least I should bake him a cake for later. I would definitely manage that, I thought. Although he had no way of knowing, money for a proper present most certainly was a problem. I wondered if he'd like a goldfish. Perhaps he'd see it as an ironic present. I doubted it.

Out of the kitchen window a blackbird in the upper branches of the crab apple exalted the glories of the golden morning. Beyond, the long grass was a froth of cow parsley. Angelica flowered in the lane. The leaves of the tree shimmered. I imagined what I'd be doing with this dewy sunlit morning if you were here with me and shivered pleasantly at the thought. Simon's present faded from view. Even through the heavy veil of guilt I only had eyes for the damp and glistening garden lit all the brighter by my burning desire to share it with you. The keys to the little Peugeot stayed wherever I'd left them. Without so much as clearing up the mess of the breakfast table I found myself striding across the soaking grass and the blackbird carried on singing.

It was just after sundown one night in April that a picture of you first slipped into my inbox attached to an email from my friend, Tilda. 'Something for the weekend?' was the subject line. Life had led Tilda down a rural path even further removed from sophistication than mine so to honour our more fabulous pasts we sometimes sent each other tantalising pictures. Our pornography, we called it: a long-running joke.

I didn't have much time to indulge myself that night, though I could see immediately that you were gorgeous, but I was already late to meet Simon and the others to celebrate the first year of the Agency. I remember he was a bit squiffy by the time we got home. We had a desultory attempt at making love but as usual he wanted the light on and I wanted it off, we tussled over the dimmer and after that sort of lost heart.

Downstairs in my dressing gown. Simon snoring the snores of a drunkard upstairs. I can remember the moment: the pulsating dome of the mouse, the blue light of the screen, the buzz of the dimmer and the hum of the fridge through the wall, and then, without knowing what I was setting in motion, I was clicking to the photograph of you that Tilda had sent. The attachment opened and my eyes locked on. It was instant and soaring, like a hot air balloon taking to the skies; it even affected my breathing. I didn't know what to do because I'd never encountered such elation before. I'd never believed in love at first sight. I was almost giddy with it. I stared at your photograph for a very long time, a fire burning within me. The next day I rekindled the same visceral heat with a second look. I was supposed to be proofreading a cookery book but I kept returning to the computer, clicking to that picture. I even Googled you. In Google Images I found some more photographs: in one you were with an Italian countess, in another a leggy blonde at the polo. I stumbled upon a whole site dedicated to your pictures. I was in good company. People had left flattering messages. They referred to your elegance, your style, and I found myself sitting up straighter, imagining my face pressed to yours. I had never felt desire like it.

The dew saturated my canvas shoes as I crossed beneath the apple trees. I would have the nuisance of having to dress up later, but for now I was free. Simon liked the usual things: dresses, high heels, underwear of the sort that comes wrapped in layers of tissue paper as though it might break. Sometimes he buys it for me, and sometimes he buys me shoes made of satin with long thin heels that say 'Manolo Blahnik' on a little name tape sewn on the instep, or even more precariously 'Jimmy Choo', cunningly pronounced 'shoe'.

Leaves glistened. The Lady's Mantle offered dewdrops. Simon always surprised me with something special – birthdays, Christmas, even our anniversary. What did I think I was doing? I stopped myself at the orchard gate. My own pleasure would have to wait. I almost turned around. Simon's present. But then the blackbird sang and my path was lit by the haze of morning sunshine. Convolvulus clung to a ruined wall, its pale green hearts hanging in strings, and my adulterously quiet, sopping wet sneakers took me closer to where you were waiting.

There had been such a heavy dewfall that the frayed hems of my jeans soon grew damp so I hoicked them up and kicked my wet shoes off into the grass. It couldn't matter to me less what I look like these days. You've opened my eyes: I'm happy to go as I please. I looked down. I could even see beauty in my bare toes, wet and streaked with brown beneath the sopping roll of my jeans. I was wearing one of Simon's old shirts, tatty at the collar from his stubble. I admit that I've become scruffier since we've been hanging around together. Simon probably despairs. Some mornings I go to put on a skirt and then my old jeans call to me from the floor where they lie discarded like an old skin with their comfortable creases, and I think how you and I will have our fun and it doesn't matter what I wear when we do.

As I crossed the orchard, I noticed that one of the top windows was latched open and a swallow flew out, so close that I could feel the breath of its wings. I felt lucky. The young swallows squeaked from their nest in the rafters where you and I once stood on tiptoe and glimpsed inside the ravenous yellow diamonds of their beaks. One morning I sneaked out here early, before the boys had even woken up, to see you. The webs that grace the windows and the door were sparkling tiaras, laced with diamonds of dew. And to think I used to let spiders go up the hoover. There's nothing like spending time in the countryside with you to make me see things in a new light.

I looked at my watch. Simon would be at work. He was probably feeling silly for caring about something as daft as a birthday present. I thought again about how often he liked to splurge on those ridiculous things for me – the watch on my wrist, the shoes in their rigid cardboard boxes. To tell the truth his presents often made me feel awkward. It's hard to remain thrilled for as long as I feel he'd like me to be, probably because I grew up in a house where above the kitchen table was a poster of a poor African child with a distended tummy and flies in his eyes. SAY NO TO WORLD POVERTY! I sometimes suspected that the better-dressed parents of my school friends, the ones with lots of scatter cushions, were the ones who said 'Yes!' to world poverty. All those wicked people with their pot-pourri and lovely soft sliced bread.

I'm stuck with much of it: brown bread and not many puddings. I fold wrapping paper to use again. I can even darn socks, something that for some reason Simon finds funny. Not so unreasonable that he should assume I'd be happy enough pickling things and making jam when we moved out here.

'Would you mind being so far from London?' he said one night, his heart already set on the fields and the trees and this cottage where everything smells of honey all summer long. I don't remember having feelings either way: as long as I was with him I would feel safe. Feeling safe was, before I met you, the only thing I'd ever wanted. A luxury I wasn't used to growing up.

'You wouldn't mind staying at home?'

I was as easy as thistledown on a summer breeze.

Before I set eyes on you I don't think I knew the meaning of true passion. One day I was quietly proofreading a book that Simon was editing, the next we were wed. Poor uncelebrated Simon, who grew up drowning in cushions and pot-pourri.

The cries of the fledglings from the rafters grew almost deafening as the swallow returned with a beakful of worm. I thought again of Simon's brave-little-soldier face this morning in the kitchen. It was an expression I knew from both Angus and Ivan. That face worked on me like the starving child of the poster.

'It's no use,' I said, detaching myself from you before we got carried away. 'I have to go.'

I was running back up the path to the kitchen, the insistent squeaks of the baby swallows ringing in my ears and my heart still pounding just from the sight of you. This had to stop.

I tipped some of the boys' cereal into a bowl and added milk. The cereal appeared to have small jelly bears in it. The jelly bears were lovely and chewy and fruity in a chemical way. Nothing so lurid ever found its way on to the breakfast table of my childhood. There, apart from the starving child poster, were pine shelves with my mother's screw-top jars with Dymo-ed labels: 'Kidney Beans', 'Mung Beans', 'Split Peas', 'Oats', row upon row of them; the world's most disappointing sweet shop.

It's the thought that counts, I decided, as I sifted through the cereal packet in search of more gummy bears, but it would have to be a very cheap thought because there was little credit left on either of my cards.

It'd be easy if I still had the money. Simon's twin brother Tim had told me which guitar shop sold them. 'The Baby Taylor.' He had been strumming his own one, tapping his foot as he played, so anyone would think he was Paco de Lucía: 'Koa wood,' he said with a smirk, nicely settled into his bachelor's throne of chrome and black leather. 'Fits in the overhead locker of any airplane.' I don't know where he imagined Simon flying off to with this guitar. But it was too late for such fantasies now. My money was spent.

It was just two days after Tilda had sent that picture that you fell into my life for real. It must have been fate. I couldn't believe my eyes when I saw you there on the other side of the glass.

Barry beckoned for me to come in, though we'd never met before. It took him just five minutes to turn my fantasy to reality. I could tell by the way he spoke that he wanted us to click.

'What have you got to lose?' he said. 'You'll never get another chance.' I wouldn't be surprised if he hides a forked tail inside those unassuming jeans of his.

I still can't quite put my finger on what it was about you that did it: the smoothness of the Hermès brown leather calf has a lot to answer for because once I'd stroked that there was no settling for anything else. Barry felt it only fair to mention the plainer, less exclusive Leica cameras, but their bodies were rough and textured. I had eyes only for you.

'A very special edition,' he said, carefully unwinding the strap. 'The Hermès Leica. Only five hundred ever made.'

He showed me the two lenses. I had already studied so many photographs of them on the internet that it was like meeting old friends. The small one with a very pleasing fifties look and the longer smooth cylinder of brushed silver with grooved dials, and a cover that slid rather suggestively back and forth along the body of the lens.

'90mm,' Barry said. 'Perfect for portraiture.'

The strap of the camera was a double ribbon of soft brown calfskin edged on both sides by lines of straight white Hermès stitches and was as flexible as living skin.

I don't know how long I stood there just staring and stroking the silky brown leather of the strap. I longed to hold that strap to my face, to wind it in bracelets around my wrists, to inhale the scent of the leather, but I could feel Barry's eyes on me. He spoke some more, about perfection.

'Number fifty-two, that's good,' he said. 'The earlier in the sequence the better.'

He hinted at investment: 'You'll be able to leave it to your children.'

There was really no need for him to say a word. My heart was beating ferociously.

The price that I imagined turned out to be hundreds of pounds short of the mark.

When I got home, trembling and slightly tearful, I didn't immediately know what to do with the great big box. The potting shed in the orchard was very much on impulse. I wrapped everything carefully in some old polythene sheets, fully intending to return it to the devil at the camera shop in the morning.

The boys both had homework that night and Tim was due for supper, which always whipped them into a bit of a froth. Later, if I hadn't been so distracted, I think I might have been able to confess all to Simon, but then I heard raised voices at the front door, the twins squabbling.

'Not Sadie.' Simon sounded upset, possibly too upset. 'Remember we all have to work together.'

Tim's voice was flustered too: 'I only said I'd meet her for a quick drink after I left here.' He cuffed Simon on the shoulder. 'It's not a date. I promised I'd help her with a bit of advice.'

'You'd better not be thinking about giving her one.' That was Simon. I shuddered and left them to it. I hated how easily Simon could zip himself back into his old bachelor-about-town skin whenever Tim was about, which was all the time at the Agency.

'Don't worry, dear,' Tim said. 'I wouldn't shit on our own doorstep.' And then the door banged.

It wasn't until the following evening that I finally got to slide your silver box out of its thick white cardboard slip case. Simon was working late and the boys were in bed.

Inside was a second box of such understated elegance that I almost gasped anew. This fine box was upholstered in the sort of taupe linen that you usually only find in very smart hotels. I lifted the lid. You were nestled on your bed of pale primrose satin. I was struck by the contrast of the soft brown leather and the hard brushed silver edges that also framed the sweet O of battery cover and the larger O for your lenses.

The lenses had their own puffy little primrose resting places beside you and there was a matching linen-covered hardback book with an embossed cover that would tell me everything I needed to know. There was a little draw-top bag of dormouse-coloured plush, a couple of zipped black leather tubes and a beige cloth as soft as a hamster's tummy for cleaning your lenses. For this little lot I had parted with every penny I had, and run up an overdraft. It made no sense at all. For some reason some words of Mary McCarthy's floated into my head as I gazed guiltily into the pale silken folds of your boudoir: 'It made no sense for me to sleep with him so I married him so it *would* make sense.' And then I knew that there was really only one thing I could sensibly do: I had to take you by the strap and get you to show me a good time.

Obviously it wasn't easy. There's a lot more to using a fully manual camera than meets the eye. At first the little linen book was enough but soon I was ushering the children out of the door and going online to the various photography sites and forums, some of which were helpful.

I learned about light and dark, shadows and flares. I started buying films by the economy dozen and became on first-name terms with the entire staff of Snappy Snaps. I was careful to stash most of my pictures in the shed but Simon occasionally, like at breakfast this morning, came across a packet and assumed I was having fun with our old pocket-sized Olympus.

I took pictures of cats for a while. I became quite a stalker of cats because we didn't have our own yet. There was a sleek black fellow who slept on a wall in Marine Parade that I practically struck up a relationship with. My pictures of that cat are among the best I've ever done: I showed them to Barry and even he said they were good.

For a couple of weeks I enjoyed taking pictures in the park, the cherry blossom was spectacular this year, but eventually I had to stop going with you there. There were too many men: on their way to work, eating sandwiches, walking dogs. 'Is that a Leica?' 'Is it the MP?' they'd ask. 'How are you finding it?' Or else they wanted to tell me about the Leicas in their lives. Some even wanted to deliver monologues about digital cameras versus film. One cheeky chap asked if he could 'cop a hold'. I hadn't realised what a man-magnet a camera could be: suddenly I understood what life must be like with a cleavage.

A couple of times I had to ask Barry for help. Eventually, having sussed that portraits and still lifes were starting to be 'my thing', he introduced me to the joys of sensitive film: 'See what you think,' he said, and then with the sly reassurance of the serpent he was: 'You'll not look back.'

I started shooting black and whites at 3200 ASA, colour at 1600. Until then most of my pictures had by necessity of light been out of doors. Being alone was the turning point. With fast film, even in failing light I could still keep my subject sharp. I could open up to a huge aperture and the tumble of books and old newspapers that I no longer quite found the time to clear up would become a background blur, a sort of Monet-esque colour wash. With nothing other than a bowl of apples between us, I started to think that every minute away from you was wasted time.

Everywhere I looked there was a picture: the sleeping profiles of the boys against their pillows, the swallows in their nest; and the ones I couldn't take, too: the dark curl of hair that escaped like a question mark where the ribbing at the neck of Simon's T-shirt had become stretched, the way his face was lit one night by the campfire he'd made for the boys in the meadow. They cooked sausages on sticks and as he leaned over the fire with Ivan's sausage the flames lit his face so he looked like James Dean and I longed for my camera to be out of the closet. I found myself working out the exposures even without the camera in my hands. How could I think about anything else? Barry, who by this point might as well have grown little red horns, had persuaded me to buy a tripod.

The tripod meant that I no longer had to stack up piles of books to steady the camera. I was able to take pictures in practically any light.

The photographs of the baby swallows came out even better than I'd expected. You could make out each individual strand of horsehair woven around their nest.

I gulped the lump in my throat. Knowing what I was about to do, I tried not to think about the swallows or the cat on the wall or any of my better photographs. There were plenty of bad ones, especially in the beginning. I was practically in a frenzy looking for my keys when Simon called.

'A babysitter?' he said. 'Do you think there's a chance someone will be free?'

Why hadn't I thought of booking her already? Obviously he'd want to go out, why hadn't I thought of it?

'Tim's reserved a table at *L'Artichaut*,' he said. I hadn't thought of that either. Hurrah for Tim.

'I think it's just us and Sadie and you.' Hearing his voice stiffened my resolve. I was going to have to be quick in town. After that it was still going to be a rush into London for the guitar shop.

Once I got to the camera shop, though, Barry had other ideas: 'Your pictures are becoming too good,' he said. 'I don't know how you could bear to part with it.'

'I must,' I said.

'You've got an eye,' he said. 'You can trade it in if you insist but you'll probably always regret it.'

Ridiculous tears were welling up in my eyes. You were tucked among your sumptuous cushions, unbearably chic; there was the linen box, the silver box, the soft leather cases. I had stored everything so carefully beneath the polythene covers that even the white slip case was pristine as new chalk. Now, as it all lay open for Barry's inspection, I had to be careful not to wet the pale primrose satin with my tears.

'It's not just what the camera's worth,' I said. 'It's the film processing. I must be up to ten a week. I can't afford to do this any more.'

'I can help you with that, at least,' Barry said. 'Where are you getting your films developed?'

I told him.

'Waste of money,' he said.

'I know.' I could've stamped my foot. 'That's why I need you to buy back this camera.'

'You don't have to pay for whole sets of prints, you know.' He told me about a woman just down the road who could make me contact sheets. 'She processes film for all the professionals; she's very good.'

I didn't know why I hadn't thought of something like contact sheets myself. It wasn't a service they offered on the high street.

'She used to be married to a photographer but he's left her,' he said. 'She's been a bit distraught.' He thought I might have heard of her: 'Her name's Morganna.'

Then he lowered his voice: 'Famous nude model in her

94

day, Morganna. You might have seen some of them, probably before your time though don't say that to her. There was
a series that Carlos Clarke shot of her with a snake. Lovely
detail of the scales and the patterns.' Beelzebub flicked out his
forked tongue, licked his lips. 'That was Morganna.'

All the time Barry was telling me this I was still holding
on to the camera. I hardly noticed her come in, until she
had passed the display cases and I could see that she had a
kind face, with the right sort of lines around her eyes and
lots of dark hair which was held back in loops and bunches
by many small silk flowers pinned hither and thither.

'Morganna, I was just talking about you.' Barry kissed
her on both cheeks and introduced me.

'This one here,' – he had rested a proprietorial hand on
my shoulder and was slightly pushing me towards her – 'this
one's taking pretty good shots with her Leica but is finding
the developing a bit pricey,' he said.

'Hello.' She glanced from me to the counter and percep-
tibly gasped: 'What a beautiful camera.' Morganna's voice was
deep like Eleanor Bron. For a moment I felt my grip tight-
ening around your brown leather body. She was gazing at
you with a look that I recognised as fervent as my own.

'I imagine they're quite rare,' she said, and her voice
seemed to have grown huskier.

I imagined this Morganna writing me out the cheque.
There'd be nothing to do but take it. She smelled expensively of rose oil and grapefruit.

'This leather is so smooth,' she said, stroking your contours
with one finger. Barry coughed.

'I think you should help her,' he said, giving my shoulder another little shake towards her. 'She's got talent.'

Barry slipped me a cable switch that had come in second-hand. 'No charge,' he whispered. 'For such a good customer.' I shook my head at him.

Morganna tore her gaze away from my camera. Her dark eyes were ringed with black kohl, precisely drawn. She studied me for a moment, unblinkingly like a cat.

'Bring me your films and I'll be happy to do contacts for you, any afternoon at three,' she said. 'Number 7 Marine Parade, at the seafront. If there's anything you like I can help you print it yourself,' she added. I felt suddenly quite thrilled at the thought of making my own prints.

'There,' said Barry, and I stopped gripping my camera so hard. 'Morganna's always been a great support to struggling artists. Now there's no need to worry.'

Morganna smiled at me like a true patron of the arts, her many bracelets jingling as she shook my hand.

The little bubble of elation that carried me home, the camera smugly in its box and not in the shop as I'd intended, burst once I remembered that I still hadn't managed a present for Simon. That morning's Snappy Snaps lay on the table where he'd left them. I got them out of the packet. They were good, it was true: the colours and the composition of Ivan and the buttercups had something of an old master painting about it. What if Barry was right and I did have talent? The late sunlight suited both Ivan's sweet, peachy-cheeked profile and the flowers in their jar at the window. The line of Ivan's eyelashes was razor-sharp and each buttercup petal seemed individually lit.

Poor Simon didn't have a clue. I almost laughed as I thought of him pontificating this morning: 'It wouldn't have occurred to me to buy a proper film since I've been doing everything on the phone,' he had said, looking at a picture where only Ivan was in focus, the jar of flowers an artful blur.

'I'd forgotten we even had a camera.' He had continued perusing another. The little automatic we'd taken on our honeymoon was in its usual place, hanging by its helpful nylon wrist strap with our coats in the hall.

'They say digital's just as good these days . . . and my Nokia's got 4.2 megapixels . . .'

I felt myself begin to yawn.

'. . . But these look better than anything I ever get with that.'

Bla, bla, bla, I wasn't really listening, but then he said that strange thing when he saw the photograph that Ivan had taken of me. Strange, but also, I now realised, rather tender.

I started with the phone. By some miracle Laura Idlewild, the boys' favourite babysitter, was not only free but agreed to stay the night. I chose my dress with care, mindful of what splendid thing might be slinked around Sadie's body in honour of Simon and Tim's birthdays. I found the most recent pair of birthday shoes, still in their box and with unblemished soles.

'Tart!' My mother's voice broke in as I buckled the ankle strap of the first shoe. 'Tart!' They were plain black; their only detail a round sparkly buckle. The shape of the buckle reminded me of the first pair I'd ever bought with my own money, though these were much nicer and satin. They'd been vinyl, the cheapest. 'Why would you want to look like a tart?' She was shaking with rage, a black platform dangling by its plastic strap like a naughty kitten from each hand. 'Who sells shoes like this to a twelve-year-old girl?' Then the march of shame back to the shop, arriving by the scruff of neck, legs dangling. 'How dare you sell her these? Refund her money right now!' The Saturday girl was Kim Nockolds; she already bullied me. 'Knuckles', she was called at school. I buckled the second satin strap around my ankle, stood up, and found to my surprise that I was able to walk in a reasonably stable fashion.

Next I booked a room with a sea view at the hotel on Marine Parade, a stroll away from *L'Artichaut*. I unrolled some sheets of greaseproof paper and masked off the sitting room window and drew the curtains until the light fell in a diffused beam across the chair.

I held you to me and there was nothing to think about but you and me and what we were about to do. You. My heart was thumping, I was starting to feel wildly elated. You'd put the spark back into my eye. I used Ivan's giant teddy bear to focus and frame.

The light was perfect: almost amber. If I was quick I would be at Morganna's by three o'clock. She would think I was a narcissist but never mind. The thought of Tim's face when Simon unwrapped my present made me laugh out loud. I started to pull off my dress.

A Regular Cherub

She had been on her haunches long enough to feel the first chill of evening rise from the brick path. Her hands busy with the Honesty, peeling seed pods, and only slightly ashamed of how pleasant it felt, doing something, anything, away from the baby. She was an Impressionist peasant picking wheat in the fields, in a lovely full skirt, not a piously suffering Madonna having to gaze for ever at one of those freaky little Jesus Christs with their prematurely adult faces. Not that her own baby had a strangely adult face, God forbid, and she didn't find him freaky. But this golden evening, when she was supposed to be already back from the chickens, she could almost believe that it was harvest time and the ache in her back had been put there by Millet.

Tilda excelled at small, fiddly work, at getting to the gleam within the gloom. As a picture restorer she had specialised in eighteenth-century miniatures and last year a trio painted in grisaille on translucent slivers of ivory, rather sentimentally, had the chopped hair of departed beloveds dissolved into the watercolour.

She peeled another pod to reveal the silicula, a disc as thin as a fish scale and silvery as a full moon. She'd added a tiny snip of her own hair to the solvent for the restoration. 'My final commission,' she'd said, sighing, when it was done, though Callum wouldn't have it: 'Plenty of people around here have pictures that need restoring,' he said. The seeds dropped away to the flowerbed. Clay soil everywhere for miles. Honesty growing like weeds.

Lunaria Annua, she'd looked it up: purple flowers in the summer, a favourite with butterflies; known also as the Money Tree or Silver Dollar because of its pods. And Honesty because of the transparency, she supposed.

She held a single peeled moon against the mauvening sky, and then closer to her eye like a monocle, but found that she couldn't see through it after all. So, really quite dishonest: not as it appeared. She stood up, stretching, and braced herself to return to the house and the baby she was supposed to love with a large chunk of her heart.

She took the branch of Honesty for Callum, its silver moons nodding as she walked up the path, but left the bowl of eggs where she'd been squatting. Her memory's not what it was: last week she left the baby's wretched car seat out in the rain and something decided to chew on it in the night. She is beginning to understand those women who say they once forgot to bring the pram home from the shops.

Callum was waiting for her in the kitchen; muddy overalls slung over the back of a chair, mucking about with the dog, a black mongrel called Bitzer. 'Bits of this, bits of that,' he said.

'And lie,' he commanded, pointing. 'Down.'

The dog dropped to the floor like an ink blot but its eyes remained fixed like a disciple on Callum's face and its heft of a tail thumped the tiles. Not even a year and already the dog sits, lies down, comes when Callum whistles and does a rolling over thing that he says is known as 'Die for the Queen', something, incidentally, that Tilda's sure neither she nor Callum would do themselves.

Milk bloomed in their mugs of tea on the table between them, and he looked so like a farmer with his raw cheeks and streaked thatch of hair that Tilda almost laughed aloud. It had been a surprisingly short road from the quasi-religious hush of Cork Street to the farm; amazing, really, that her feet had kept up. Only a year since he'd have come home in a suit with real cufflinks and she'd been the scruff in her turpentine-reeking smock.

'Lie and die for the Queen,' Callum said.

At this rate it wouldn't be long before he had a straw sticking out of his mouth and he'd be whistling hymns by Charles Wesley.

'I think I missed my vocation,' he said, rubbing Bitzer's ears.

For a moment she thought she'd been thinking out loud and he meant the whistling.

'Don't you think I'd have made a great dog trainer?'

There were many things she could have said to this, shrewish things about the farm: about the stink, the middle-of-nowhere stink; muck spreading; leaky silage pit; the mud and muddle of it all. So many things sprung to mind, most of them brown.

'Dog shit would be the cherry on the cake,' she said, and they both found themselves momentarily transfixed with that image and laughed, so in the end they didn't have to trudge up the usual conversational cul-de-sac of the farm versus their old flat in Hackney.

'Danny's due to get up again when you've drunk that.' Callum snatched a glance at the clock and a gulp of tea. The tea was far hotter than she could ever manage, and the clock, like most of the furniture in the farmhouse, was his mother's, fixed high on the whitewash above the sink, from where its neon hands kept them in check. Wake, milk, nappy, it was unrelenting: nappy, milk, sleep, with the yawning stretches of time in between when she wasn't sure what she was meant to be doing with the ubiquitous baby.

'You might need to wake him, or he'll be a devil to get back to sleep later.' Callum nagged, but only gently. He stuck his fingers through his hair and gave her his we're-in-this-together smile. Not for the first time she wished that she could take the baby's batteries out. Maybe only for a day or two. She'd be better if she could have a rest.

She handed Callum the branch she'd brought, its moons shimmering.

'Very pretty,' he said. 'What is it?'

'You must know, it grows everywhere.' She was surprised. 'You're the one who grew up here.'

'My mother was a proper farmer's wife.' He was teasing her. 'Far too busy pickling medlars and digging up swedes, not much time for flower arranging.'

'Too busy skinning rabbits, more like,' she said.

'With her teeth,' Callum added, making Tilda giggle.

'Drinking milk straight from the cow,' she said.

'Milking the bull.'

'Ugh,' Tilda cuffed him lightly on the shoulder, 'now you've gone too far.' Callum could be so disloyal about his mother. Sometimes it really helped.

'I reckon Jane's been too busy killing foxes to manage anything else recently,' said Tilda.

This was partly true. Her mother-in-law had, since the anti-hunting bill was passed, taken to using her shotgun with a vengeful finger on the trigger, as though it was the foxes themselves who had cast the votes in Parliament. Tilda put down her tea and tried not to dwell on something Jane had told her that morning, the thought of it still making her queasy.

At eight-thirty a.m. prompt, a gust of dust and a pair of brown and white terriers quarrelling about which should get through the door first had announced Jane's arrival. She was on her way between the bungalow that she referred to rather grandly as 'The Dower House' and the yard. Tawny-haired, with a feverish high-colour undimmed by recent widowhood, she was eager to get the job done. Jane had plenty of time for getting the job done now that the fun had been taken out of the fox-hunting: 'Galloping around after some boy trailing a wee-soaked rag from a quad bike.' She said she really couldn't abide it, especially since the futility of it all 'makes the hounds look so stupid'.

'Here, I brought this for the boy.' She stood a large and rather morose maroon velvet bear with leather-soled feet on the table, bunched up her chins to study it. Its nose and ears showed the balding downside of having once been loved.

'Callum's,' she said. It looked lumpy, like it might be stuffed with sawdust or straw. Jane glanced at Danny in his

105

playpen finishing his breakfast: a fat pasha surrounded by a harem of much friendlier creatures. 'In the cage again, I see,' she said.

Tilda baulked, changed the subject: the farm cat. 'About the tabby . . .' She'd seen it in the hay barn, making a nest in the straw. It had growled at her when she got close. 'I think it's about ready to burst.'

Jane was at the table counting out sachets, some sort of powdered antibiotic that came in a large red box.

'Have you homes for the kittens?' Tilda asked.

Jane finished counting, flipped an elastic band around the bundle, wrote something in the veterinary log. 'Don't need homes.' She dropped the pen into her bag. 'The dogs will take care of that.'

'What?' A momentary lapse. Then acid in Tilda's mouth. 'Jane, that's disgusting.'

Danny paused from smearing banana along the bars of his playpen and started to whimper.

'That's nature,' Jane retorted, snapping the book shut.

Tilda put the Honesty into a blue spotted jug, placed it in the centre of the table.

'Tilly, it really is about time to wake Danny up.' Callum again. 'Do you want me to go? Do you think he'll be grumpy if he's expecting you?'

Callum was always itching to see Danny whenever he managed to break free from the unrelenting lactation and the constant slurry of the cowsheds. Tilda didn't mention the cat. She looked at him and she looked at the way he stroked the worn head of the maroon bear that he'd found waiting for him on the table and it dawned on her that this farming thing wasn't a phase; it was more than just a few years of helping the family out: it was in his system. The rhythms set by dawn and dusk ran through his veins, the total darkness and well-earned slumber; she'd never known him happier. He loved the clear night skies and the Milky Way, the misty dawns and the way the farmhouse was cut into the hill and the long shadows of the old trees. He was in the fold to stay: a good son.

Rooting about in the desk earlier that day, Tilda had come across Jane's letter, had re-read it, trying to remind herself what tempting bait had been concealed within its seven Manila pages when it was sent to them in Hackney: it must've been something tasty, for how else had she managed to reel them in like this?

She had written mainly about the particular breed of cow in residence on the farm: Tilda had been mistaken in thinking them fairly ordinary black and white ones, for according to this magnum opus, Jane's cows had a splendid family tree with its roots in the days when Thomas Sidney Cooper painted in the meadows. Callum's Great-great-grandfather Samuel started this line of cows and it had remained unbroken through two world wars. 'And such a high milk yield,' she wrote. Erroneously, as it turned out.

Then, astonishingly, tucked away in its own paragraph on page five: 'I think your child should grow up on the farm.' Callum had sworn that he hadn't mentioned the pregnancy: they'd agreed to wait before telling *anyone*; after all Danny was still no more than a small prawn then.

'And Tilda could find plenty here to do.' Tilda was surprised she hadn't suggested she paint portraits of the cows. Whatever. His father's health was failing and Callum, she made it clear, would be needed on the farm before calving season.

'I grew up there,' he said. 'It'll be easy for me to feel at home; I'm trained for it already.' He claimed that Cork Street was making him cynical, giving him migraines: 'Too much bad art,' he said. 'And you'll have the baby, the air will be better for the baby.'

'There was a piece today in *The Times* about happiness,' she said one evening, the baby safely stowed in his cot, she and Callum companionable with a basket between them on the table, shelling walnuts she'd brought, heads almost touching, their fingers staining brown.

She had found the walnuts in the nettles, fallen all around the tree beyond the kitchen garden, and what was left of summer's Honesty, not much more than twigs, a few pods mottled with mildew, too battered by the wind to give up their moons. She collected the nuts, cursing the nettles, and then shook a branch of the tree and more came raining down, hard on her head like the rapping of knuckles; a punishment, like the nettle stings on her wrists, for not loving her baby.

'*The quest for happiness is a national disease.*'

Callum pulled out a chair and rested a leg on it, hinging himself back and forth over it, easing his back. 'Why should anyone *expect* to be happy?' he said. She raised her eyebrows: it was the sort of thing his mother would say. 'How do you find the time to read all this stuff anyway?'

'I know, I know,' she said, irritated, and then in Jane's exasperated tones: 'Failing to get that baby out in the fresh air.'

'Actually, Danny's got a bit of a snuffly snotty nose,' said Callum.

She started scrubbing some large potatoes for their supper, under the water that always felt colder than the water she was used to in town. He put his arms around her and nuzzled her neck. 'Sorry,' he said.

The happiness survey, she told him, was based on several hundred people who went about wired up to a little machine that bleeped at random times of the day and night. When it bleeped they had to enter a number between one – miserable – and ten – ecstatic – for how they felt at that moment and type in what they were up to at the time.

'In the end it didn't really matter what people were actually doing but everyone was at their happiest when concentrating.'

She was thinking about the long hours she'd spent under the lights in Cork Street moving between the microscope and the fine slivers of ivory; her total absorption, the little rubber bungs in the bottles, the tiny brushes and Q-tips.

'The workers on the production line were no more or less happy than the poets.'

She thought too of how she'd managed to grasp a similar sort of happiness in recent evenings, before the weather turned, alone in the vegetable garden, the baby mercifully keen on long afternoon naps, pretending she was fetching herbs for the supper, or potatoes to dig, but really squatting down and peeling away at the Honesty as if her living depended on it. She had armfuls of the stuff, enough for the biggest jug, more. It was a hard-earned break, usually. The baby, never easy to settle, always called her back, again and again. She started to cut the potatoes into thin slices; she'd bake them in a sauce of the walnuts with mushrooms and cream. Maybe, she suddenly thought, it wasn't concentrating that made you happy; perhaps being focused on something simply distracted you from being sad.

Callum wondered how he'd grade fixing the tractor that morning. 'Definitely no more than a five,' he said. He leaned against the Aga rail. He was not really built for heavy work: his long back made him vulnerable to strain. He reminded Tilda of a sad clown in his baggy clothes with his hair sticking up like that and she wished she could stop herself from needling him, but it was hard after a day with the baby, after another morning listening to his mother.

'It wasn't an awful lot of fun getting covered in oil but I was definitely concentrating on the bugger,' he said.

She unwrapped paper from around some lamb chops: they came from a neighbouring farm; all their meat did, in return for milk. He sipped his tea and then perked up, literally brushing down his trousers, in the way that a child picks himself up after a fall.

'Anyway eventually I got it working so I was happy,' he said.

'You're a much better man than me.' Tilda moved towards him for a hug, but Callum cocked his ear at the door to the stairs, in the way that let her know that he'd heard Danny cry, as usual before she'd heard him herself.

He opened the door with a small bow and a gentlemanly sweep of his arm, gesturing for her to step through it.

Tilda pinched him as she passed and clumped up the wooden stairs to find her bawling child.

Danny had finally come into the world, after almost ten months' gestation, at Teign Hospital, a terrifying fifteen miles from the farm. Had Callum's truck not chosen that night to have an ignition failure, they would never have thought to ask his mother to deliver them to the maternity suite. Driving wasn't one of Jane's strong points. It was two o'clock in the morning so luckily there wasn't too much other traffic as she weaved indiscriminately on both sides of the road, tyres squealing in mad pursuit of every rabbit that had the misfortune to be lit by her headlights. 'Run 'em down,' she said, and Tilda, in the back, biting Callum's hand with each contraction in an effort to 'buck up', would not have been surprised had she started blowing on a bugle.

Tilda's first thought when she set eyes on Danny was of a Christmas gammon, boiled and ready for studding with cloves. His eyes were rimmed and sore-looking, almost myxomatosis rabbit. She stared with a rather queasy and complicated fascination at the livid creature, with its flailing arms and the umbilical cord, like a great purple worm still attached to its tummy, and knew that these were not the thoughts she was supposed to be having.

'When Callum was born I couldn't believe the overwhelming currents of love that flowed from me to him,' Jane said. 'I would have killed anyone who came near', and Tilda stared at the baby as it was laid, still screaming and slimy with blood, on to her stomach. She bit her lip and thought that now she was going to be found wanting at this along with everything else.

Tilda had read about deep eye contact, or 'imprinting' if you're a poultry breeder; she had witnessed it on the farm dozens of times with the cows giving birth. She had stood in the barn and listened to the soft sounds they made calling to their calves as they emerged with an almighty squelch on to the straw; shiny and streaked in their slick blue sac of membranes. The mothers nuzzled and licked, miraculously turning them from slimy sea creature (that no matter how many times you witnessed it you always believed must be dead), to fluffy toy-shop thing on drunken legs, a magical transformation achieved with no other trick than the steady caress of their tongues.

The cows were clearly superior beings. Tilda didn't feel the need to stare at her baby in quite such a star-struck way. In fact as he lay there slithering on her stomach, she was ashamed to remember that she had looked around the room, as though she was seeing it for the first time; the calming tone of the pale green walls, the tasteful stripe of the curtains, and wondered about the other mothers. How many births had the room seen? How many didn't make it out?

They decided to call him Danny, which was about the only name from Callum's list that Tilda hadn't vetoed on the grounds of being characters in novels by Thomas Hardy. Jane was disappointed, naturally, when 'Samuel' was not chosen. 'Such a fine family name.'

'Oh Danny boy,' Callum whistled as they drove to the farm, Tilda with the newborn in swaddling, as recommended by Jane; trying to feel something more than pity, still believing that the love would come crashing in along with her milk.

She kept waiting. The eye contact business didn't improve. It seemed to Tilda that there was always something she didn't want to see. He had sticky eye at a week old; all that yellow crustiness made her own eye feel gummy just to look at it, and the health visitor suggested she squirt a little milk into it from her breast. And now he was at eye level in the high chair, sitting up and burbling, she was scared that if she looked she might find reproach. It was all beginning to feel too late. She sang 'You Are My Sunshine' and 'I've Got You Under My Skin', but didn't mean a word.

She'd tried to brush everything away with jokes when he was new: 'Quite honestly, I'd rather go out in the garden and dig worms', when the health visitor called, a crash course in the fine art of feeding, 'I'd be good at finding worms.' All that talk of aiming the areola to the back of Baby's mouth. 'Do it so he nearly gags!' Her breast grappled with like something to be stuffed into the gaping cavity of a chicken.

Stout in Hush Puppies, the health visitor had been a daily occurrence. She brought green cabbage leaves when Tilda was so inflamed that her breasts looked like two monstrous gorgonzolas, cornflower for her cracked nipples and, on Fridays, iced buns for Callum.

After the first few weeks Jane took to calling in when the health visitor was due, and discussions of Tilda's nipples took place in the other room, over a cup of tea. They noticed when Tilda's breasts had leaked into a pillow. Perhaps the boy had missed a feed? Tilda began to feel that she belonged in the dairy. If she didn't watch out they'd call in the vet. Eventually she gave up and put the baby on the bottle. The first night she dreamt that her breasts were two scoops of melting vanilla ice cream, the second night was more disturbing: she dreamt that her mother-in-law came into the room wearing her maternity bra, dancing and swaying, opening and shutting the flaps, up and down, flaunting it.

By the time of Callum's birthday Danny had started on solids. 'A one-man chimpanzee's tea party,' Callum called it, laughing at the mess, though Tilda secretly dreaded the mashed and mouled food reappearing later in the folds of Danny's neck. She had gift-wrapped for Callum the new Halliwell's, though they hadn't seen a film for ages, and an American first edition of *In Cold Blood* that she'd found at the village bookshop, as well as the sheepskin-lined water-proof boots that he had asked for and she thought hideous.

She had dragged herself out of bed before he stirred, to arrange his presents on the kitchen table and to get the kettle boiling. Danny was already squawking, of course, so she grabbed him on her way down. 'Blimey,' she said when she got to the kitchen and Jane's clock. 'Five bloody a.m.'

'He'll make the perfect farmer.' Jane always said that about Danny. 'The hours he keeps. It's in his blood, you know . . .'

Didn't she know it. Tilda lodged the infant farmer on the mat at her feet, changed his nappy and tried not to gag as she wiped him clean with a wad of damp kitchen roll. Danny kicked his fat legs and rolled himself over. She wondered if all babies had that much cellulite on their bottoms as he did lewd little press-ups in an effort to master the mechanics of crawling away.

The day stretched before her: a day with Danny was like being left in charge of a nuclear power plant, lonely and bleak, slightly nerve-racking, with lots of servicing and safety checks required. Cal would be down any minute, dressed in his usual garb plus extra-thick socks over his jeans, and the grey beanie hat that he'd taken to wearing. Happy Birthday to You. Later Jane would galumph by for

114

her coffee morning and a madly gesticulated monologue on the Meet down at Southwood; the fall she'd taken from her horse, the way she'd got straight back into the saddle. 'Tough as old boots, me,' she'd say.

Another day with Danny. Too wet to go out. She could already hear the wind whining between the barns, driving straight at them from the East. 'Siberia.' She shivered, remembered a map of the winds from geography lessons at school. All arrows pointing at good old Blighty. It was still dark outside and the bare knuckles of climbing plants battered the kitchen windows.

Cream for their porridge, a golden swirl of demerara in the shape of a heart in his bowl. Six o'clock in the morning and Callum had already opened his presents. Danny was in his father's arms, chewing on the corner of the first edition of Truman Capote's masterpiece.

'I've decided to make you a cake,' she said.

'It's easier to make a baby than a cake, you know. Wouldn't you rather?' He looked to the ceiling in the direction of their bedroom. 'It's quicker, more fun . . .' Callum had four younger brothers; she could have seen this coming. Jane was the eldest of eight. Theirs was a family that liked to breed.

'It's certainly quicker,' she retorted, retrieving the Capote from harm but making Danny howl in the process, and Callum flicked her backside with the tea towel.

Callum wasn't wrong. It had been easier, and a lot more fun, to make a baby than a cake: they'd done it without even trying.

Making the cake was more of a performance. Having to fit it in around Danny's mucky new menu, and finding the

115

time to drive into town for baking powder and icing sugar and candles. Having to chat to busybodies.

Danny in the front of the trolley like any other baby.

A voice in her ear: 'Well, he looks nothing like you, dear, does he?' Turning to find a large woman in an unseasonally floral dress. Danny, slumped down a bit too far into the trolley seat, his face concertinaed into his chins, the familiar bullfrog pose. He looked like Jane. She remembered someone saying that all children closely resembled one of their grandparents more than any other ancestor.

Tilda hauled Danny up in the seat, managed her usual, 'No, he doesn't, does he? I think my husband must've had an affair!' The woman laughed, reached in to touch the baby's cheek, as they all did. 'With himself,' she added.

The woman withdrew her hand from Danny's cheek. 'You take good care of him, mind,' she said, and studied Tilda for a little longer than was comfortable, leaving Tilda with the feeling that somehow this woman *knew*.

The cake she made from two mounds of Victoria sponge, beautifully iced and smoothed in vanilla fondant: a pair of breasts. Her own, obviously. It would be like handing them back to him. She had been thinking about it all day, about how she'd ice it and colour it; and then she'd got Danny to sleep a whole extra half-hour, just time to add the nipples in chocolate icing and change out of her mucky jeans.

Callum strode in whistling a hymn. He'd hired a new hand, what a relief. A Quaker, as it happened, so he'd be good at silence.

He laughed when he saw his cake, blew out the candles, but it was as Tilda was cutting it, Danny safely decanted upstairs in his cot, that he got his birthday wish: a final furious howl of wind, something that sounded like a door slamming, and then black. Perfect timing. Not even a moon.

Callum put a match to the first candle, his face flared almost manically above it, gleaming skin and dark eyes shining, burnished and bronzed as a painting by Georges de La Tour. Tilda reached across the table and stroked his cheek. His smile was conspiratorial, his teeth very white by candlelight.

'There, this is something you only get here. Total blackness and silence.' He smiled broadly, the love of a good power cut. Next he'd have to build up the fire, light another in their bedroom; primitive pleasures, she supposed, candles all over the place. 'Caveman,' she said, returning his smile.

They heard the front door clatter. 'Callum, you'd better come.' A blast of cold air. She was very sorry, she said. If Callum didn't finish fitting the spare parts to the generator in the next couple of hours they'd be out of battery juice before the morning. 'Come now,' she rasped again, breathless from her journey, borne by the wind across the fields. 'Unless, of course, you fancy milking all the ladies yourself by hand in the morning.'

Tilda waved goodbye to their bath by candlelight. Callum stuck the candle to a saucer and she fumbled in the kitchen drawer for the tinfoil and covered the bosoms.

'I'll leave Bitzer,' Callum said, pulling on his big grey coat, kissing her apologetically. 'Stay,' he commanded. He thought she might get 'freaked out' alone in the dark.

Unsurprisingly Bitzer didn't settle without Callum. She

could see him dimly across the room, nose pressed to the door, pining for his master like Greyfriars Bobby. Lucky she liked to be alone, she thought, the way things were around here. Except she wasn't really alone, was she? Danny was asleep upstairs, how could she have forgotten? She thought about the woman in the shop, the look she'd given her. She would never tell anyone the truth. Not her mother, not her sister, not any of her friends, least of all Callum. What sort of woman doesn't love her own child? She can't even make herself love him. She's tried: it's like willing a dream.

She found herself moulding the top of the candle, a face of warm wax, molten tears dripping down, and then she heard it: something on the stairs, a sort of scrabbling, and Bitzer barked and leapt up.

Taking a candle and another in her pocket, she called the dog to come with her. Again, that sound. Her own shadows spooked her up the stairs, flickering on the ochreous walls and umber wood, a hunchback, stooped over the flame with a hand cupped around it. The dog followed her as she listened, cocking his head to one side. She could hear only the wind rattling the landing windows, battering the corrugated roof of the feed-store a bit further away.

Tilda held the candle above her sleeping son. He was curled around Callum's old maroon velvet bear. She could see, objectively, that Danny was a regular cherub with his blowzy cheeks and vigorous curls, his thumb resting on his lower lip. She stared for a while and then turned and checked the window.

She placed the saucer with the candle on the nursery dresser and lit another from it. She lifted the old velvet bear from the cot and stood it high on the dresser shelf. She tucked the knitted blanket around Danny. Bitzer, the creep, had already deserted her to await his master's voice. Cursing him, she took her new candle and carried it quickly downstairs with her hand cupped around it before the shadows started their dance.

As she rounded the bottom steps something flashed past her on its way up, a silver wraith of a thing, then gone. The tabby cat. Tilda remembered with a pang that she had meant to do something to save the kittens. Too late now.

She had been back downstairs for over an hour, it might well have been two. She didn't like to dwell on it. She had been sketching the shadows of the room with a piece of charcoal from the fire, the narrowest rib of a moon at the window.

The first thing she noticed when she awoke in the chair was the smell. She checked the fireplace before anything else, then the Aga. Then she was up the wooden stairs, the smell of burning getting stronger, and running along the corridor. It was advancing towards her along the ceiling, a dark fist uncurling from the door of Danny's room. She couldn't remember grabbing him, just the louring smoke hanging above his cot, a cloud slipping down over a mountain. Somehow she must have got the window open and chucked out the smouldering remains of the velvet bear and the flaming nursery cushions and made it with Danny, crushed to her, down the stairs without her legs giving way beneath her.

Back in the kitchen, Tilda collapsed on to a chair with Danny in her arms. His eyes were closed, his lashes long against his cheek. She squeezed him closer and looked down into his beautiful face. Translucent in the candlelight

119

like polished ivory, a delicate wash of pink over his cheeks, the juicy-redcurrant curve of his lip still dented by his thumb, a head full of golden curls, a regular cherub. Beloved. He was breathing steadily, his head against her chest, asleep though her heart was hammering. He opened his eyes and looked up into hers. Light flickered in his dark pupils. She heard the front door open but couldn't tear her eyes away. A warmth like candlelight ran through her. He reached a hand to her cheek and rested it there, calming her.

This is how Callum found them when he returned. Beside them, on the table, was the jug of Honesty, glowing golden planets, the single flame finding the gleam within the gloom in the unlit room.

Morganna

Morganna burst into my life, jingling and jangling armfuls of bracelets and puffing thin cigarettes that she rolled herself, silk flowers scattered here and there in twists of dark hair, fresh from her crisis and still prone to sudden tears. My shoulders were not the kind that usually got cried on: a bit on the tense side, I suppose, what with Simon working all the time and Angus and Ivan like leaky buckets, never full no matter how much I poured into them.

Morganna's fandango. What a nightmare. Things being thrown: hot cups of tea across the kitchen, Mike's clothes into Marine Parade, the photographs of their wedding day removed from the top of the piano, put back again, twice, and removed again with such force that the glass shattered in the frames.

She was wild when he left: a river of tears washing over a fortnight's dismal blow jobs that failed to make him stay.

She put half a brick through the window of the basement he was renting one night when he wouldn't open the door. His girlfriend Elizabeth, who he pretended didn't live there with him at all, looked up from playing her oboe, straight at Morganna outside on the pavement, and, laying the oboe carefully down, raised her arms to release a long skein of hair from its band, sending it falling and swinging down her back like molten metal, and sashayed to the telephone to call the police.

Morganna's driving is not improved when she tells me about these things.

I had, though not without misgiving, agreed to put my life in Morganna's hands a couple of afternoons a week. She was quite bold when she suggested it:

'Mike did all the driving,' she told me one afternoon when I'd come with my films to the studio she ran from the basement of her house. 'After twenty-nine years in the passenger seat I'll be needing to brush up.'

Her house in Marine Parade was full of stuff: cats and oriental rugs and pictures and mirrors and ancient masks on the wall, and that was just what I managed to glimpse on my way from the front door to the basement. She even had a parrot in a brass cage.

I was there to collect a print she'd made of one of my photographs, from a series of black and whites I'd shot of my cat with a vole swinging from his mouth. I'd managed to capture the medallion-man swagger of the moment, we both agreed. It was hand-printed, silver lith. Morganna held it up so I could admire it, before slipping it between sheets of corrugated green plastic.

'It's come out well,' she said and taped my negative to the

outside. 'So, I was wondering, would you let me drive your car?' It was so abrupt I thought I might have misheard her. 'A few times, for the practice,' she said, looking at me with her head on one side. 'Just until I remember how it's done.'

Morganna had been raised by half-baked Maoists in a hippy town called Totnes where favours were traded with tokens in the shape of acorns, so bartering was second nature to her. I was taken aback because I hardly knew her but she had a generous face that I liked, large features; grave eyes almost raccoon-like with the amount of dark eye make-up she piled on, a habit of biting the corner of her lip when she smiled her easy smile and a laugh that promised mischief.

'What do you think? In return I'll develop your stuff free of charge.' I'd been getting through a lot of films, more than I could really afford to have developed, and Morganna had taken quite a fancy to my little Peugeot 305. I liked her voice, too, it was husky from the roll-ups. 'The aromatherapists outnumbered the plumbers by about a thousand to one, the Acorn Economy wasn't without its problems,' she said, taking a pinch of tobacco and sliding a liquorice paper across the tip of her tongue.

'I never even got to touch the radio in our car and the steering wheel was most definitely out of bounds,' she said, the first time she sat clutching my car's wheel. 'I'm sure I *could* drive . . . I have definitely got a licence and I can remember taking a red Mini Moke right up the middle of Portobello Market . . .'

I was in awe of her then. I was nervous when she developed my films and printed my pictures, worrying that my composition was not good or the exposures ill-judged; she made prints for the best of them. There was glamour to her, she was festooned with it: all those bracelets she wore, the layers of fine fabrics, the charms and old meaningful rings that hung from her neck, clustered together on a long gold chain, the hints of a rackety life once lived up and down the Kings Road.

I called for her on Tuesdays and Thursdays at two-thirty in the afternoon so we had a clear hour to mow down pedestrians before I had to collect my pair of leaky buckets from their school. The mornings would have suited me just as well but she told me she was still finding it hard to raise herself; what with the great weight of her soul pressing on her chest as soon as she opened her eyes, so heavy, she said, it felt like it had been ripped from her in the night and plonked there, filled with rubble.

She often spoke of her soul until I imagined it louring down on her in her silk-swagged chamber, heavy and bowed with grief. A long candle burning and through the bay windows a view all the way to the horizon, only a road and the promenade between the former marital bed and the ocean. That black soul engulfing the clouds of silver-threaded tresses on her pillow, and seeping over the tragedy of her throat, so swan-like in Mike's celebrated pictures of once upon a time; her eyes smudged by yesterday's kohl. How could he leave her so sad? In the autumn, when he knew how she dreaded the winter each year. After a lifetime.

Talk at home was all tractors, Lego and Cheestrings, three sevens are twenty-one and the thrilling adventures of Biff and Chip, only the occasional grunt or sigh from

Simon. My cat had more to say than my husband these days and now that the more unpredictable brick-throwing phase was over, a couple of episodes a week of Morganna's drama was, I came to realise, just what the doctor ordered.

Though Morganna claimed her soul was in torment she never failed to cheer me up.

Sometimes I could feel my poor Peugeot quake. A variety of stimuli could set Morganna off: an alabaster statuette spied through his window, flaunting its nakedness atop his new desk: 'Do you suppose it reminds him of *her*?' CDs. A book spotted lying on the back seat of his car, a thick one with an irritating title: 'The man on the cover looked to be in fear of his life,' she said, rattling my keys at the ignition irritably.

'What's he doing reading self-help books?'

I had more or less given up trying to dissuade Morganna from making these detours up Mike's road. Her innocent request for driving practice had very soon taken on a *Thelma & Louise*-style urgency all of its own. Our route usually took us by his flat and there were forays past his studio down by the lighthouse too, where occasionally she parked with a vantage point to his assistant carrying lighting rigs in and out. Shamefully, we often took off along the seafront to pass the rehearsal hall where Elizabeth sometimes went to play her oboe. The one time we saw her walking along the street, oh, it was a carefree, pony-tail-swinging sort of a walk, Morganna squealed like a schoolgirl with a crush and ducked down into her own lap, despite the fact that she was the one who was actually driving, and I had to grab the wheel or we would have crashed.

Sometimes, Morganna told me, she couldn't sleep at night and in the darkness she tiptoed, quite undetected, through the perfumed gardens of Elizabeth's Facebook. Elizabeth seemed to have accepted Morganna's alter ego as a friend. I said it just proved how few friends she had in the real world.

Bang outside Mike's flat and into a space either directly behind or directly in front of his car always seemed to Morganna to be the perfect place to practise parking. The curtains were drawn at the front, they had been since the last time he'd allowed her over the threshold and, much to Elizabeth's displeasure and Morganna's later mortification, she and Mike had ended up wrestling on the floor like bad children.

Once parked, Morganna was able to nip out and search for those little sharp nuggets of information that she so craved, peering through the windows of his black Audi. I watched her with her hands against the glass of the car that had once been her chariot and cringed as I imagined Elizabeth or Mike seeing her there.

'*Awaken the Giant Within!* What's that supposed to mean? When did he ever read books like that?' She huffed, as we pulled away in a series of ostrich jerks.

'Mirrors, mirrors!' I yelled.

'Silly little girl must be telling him what to read! Self-help!' Her bracelets jangled as she thumped the steering wheel for emphasis: 'He never had any trouble helping himself!' Ignoring the hooting from the car behind.

'What do you suppose I did to his giant anyway to put it to sleep?' She scraped the gears as she changed into third. 'Sorry,' she said to me, and to the man who'd overtaken, shaking his head. 'And he's listening to The Ting Tings! What's he doing listening to The Ting Tings?'

A regular prompt to her misery was parked in the drive beside her house. It was her only vehicle: a purple camper van of such pastel perfection that I'd have begged, stolen or borrowed it in a heartbeat.

'I can't afford driving lessons,' she said, and grinned foolishly. 'I call her Lucille.' She was shining the chrome cone of a wing mirror with the end of her sleeve. 'Silly to give her a name, isn't it?'

Lucille deserved a name. She was vintage with the soft contours of patisserie, icing the exact colour of Parma Violets with cream fenders and wheel arches and cream leather upholstery. I couldn't imagine that Morganna's driving would ever be up to taking the driver's seat but couldn't help but envy her the dream.

'Years restoring it, Mike turned quite nutty doing it,' she said the first time she showed me inside. 'You wouldn't believe how many specialists it's been to, how many beauty treatments she's had: re-chromers, re-upholsterers, re-veneerers, his attention to detail down to the last screw; the full facelift, you name it.'

Lucille had been Mike's present to Morganna. Inside there was a leopard-skin rug for the bed, enamel plates in pastel colours and gold stars painted on the dark purple ceiling.

'Our plan was to drive Route 66,' she said, pulling out a drawer and showing me the slim cutlery stacked side by side and the clever salt and pepper pots shaped like two little figures hugging one another.

There wasn't money available to buy a car; she could

hardly pay the electricity bill now Mike had gone. And all the professionals were turning to digital. She'd once had an unpleasant experience with a mini-cab driver so was understandably a little phobic. Life would be a hassle if she didn't drive something and I couldn't see that she would ever part with Lucille.

At least she didn't have to worry about the house. Her sedate grandmother, a duchess or something similar, had bypassed the half-baked Maoists in favour of the only grandchild and Morganna inherited number 7 Marine Parade, in all its decayed elegance and glory, the day she turned eighteen.

She'd remained there ever since, wildly for a while and then settled: Mike, the children, pets, a piano. Now she rattled about its various rooms with nothing but the increasingly decrepit pets for company and Mike seemed happy to live in a basement. I had been outside this dull basement too many times. It was like watching a drug addict as she tried to wean herself off passing his – his and Elizabeth's – door, was pleased if she ever managed not to go there; her hands with ideas all of their own gripped the wheel, turning her right instead of staying straight, however hard she tried to will them not to.

'Focus on what you're doing before you kill someone!' I yelled as we skidded to a halt, and the gentleman who was halfway over the zebra crossing thumped my bonnet.

'You are the one who is actually driving the car,' I told her for the umpteenth time.

She explained that whenever we were driving close to his flat she was swept up by a salty great wave of nostalgia and longing, as though the steering wheel was his penis; it was the exact girth and smoothness apparently, that and the particular texture of the grey vinyl that Peugeot had used in my 305.

I planned to buy one of those furry things to cover it as soon as I could.

She admitted that it was self-harm, obsessive-compulsive, a way of staying connected, addictive. She went online every evening and analysed the transactions in his bank and credit card accounts because she still had the passwords. He was taking holidays in Santorini and the Spanish mountains. He had spent two hundred and fifty-six pounds at Dinny Hall the jeweller. She imagined him and Elizabeth on the mountain bikes they'd taken to riding everywhere – though she'd always found it difficult to get him to even go for a walk – freewheeling between the banks of flowers that lined the pass, light as the wind. She practised small dis-courtesies: ripping up his final parking fine reminders and his *Photography Magazine* subscription renewal notices that still came to her house.

It was her second summer without Mike and still she was at it: spending precious sunshine looking at the many flat-tering photographs that Elizabeth had posted of herself on her own website. Elizabeth irritatingly listed her many achievements: prizes at the Royal Music College, recitals, a couple of pop projects that seemed to involve her wear-ing a negligee to play.

Morganna's torture of choice featured Elizabeth with her long curtains of hair hanging each side of her face, slightly over-exposed so her skin was the very essence of ivory soap and her large, extravagantly – 'falsely!' – lashed eyes straight to camera, the rings of his flash showing in her pupils. It was a studied, brilliantly chiaroscuro portrait that Mike had taken the first time he'd set his eyes on her. A commission for a colour supplement line-up of young musicians. Her lips were around a long Japanese instrument called a shakuhachi. 'Japanese slang for blow job!' she was quoted as saying in the piece when it was published, thus guaranteeing herself the largest photograph of the bunch.

'Overblown view of her own talent,' Morganna said. 'Her and her perfect little embouchure.'

Mike left Morganna on a late September evening, just before Lola, their last child, departed for university, ensuring that Lola was the one who had ultimately to leave Morganna completely alone in her big empty house at Marine Parade. Elizabeth was the love of his life, he said. What else could he do? He had to take his chance for happiness.

At first he said he'd do nothing to hurt Morganna but that changed along with the weather. Adrenalin and loneliness were not a pretty cocktail and he couldn't fail to notice how thin she was becoming, how drawn her face looked in the grey winter afternoons. Every night as he gazed into the face of an angel on the pillow beside him in the cosy basement, he persuaded himself that Morganna was a demon who had brought this all upon herself. Employing the sort of tactics that one country's government will use to justify bombing another, he publicised her shortcomings. To their friends he said she once threw a fork at him and it stuck in his chin.

'Yes,' said Morganna. 'We even managed to laugh at the time. It was an accident. He makes it sound like I stabbed him.'

To Lola he confessed that he couldn't remember ever having been happy in the marriage and Lola, so proud of her own resistance, stupidly told Morganna on the phone what he'd said and how in response she had stuck to her resolve regarding Elizabeth. She was away from it all at university: 'I said that I didn't want her turning up with him here,' she said, good for her, but Morganna had been left stumbling about in the bombsite of this thing she'd just been told, half blind, and all the bits of shrapnel from the earlier explosions still working their way out. Lola delivering a fresh wound, and a deep one. 'Never happy. What, really, *never*?'

The aftershocks every bit as bad: one day deleting his voice on their answerphone and the next regretting it so bitterly that she'd asked him, pathetically, if he would do her a new one, she thought it would be better if a burglar called. 'Any man's voice would do,' he said, putting down the phone.

The problem was that it was still 'his' voice whenever she got him to pick up the phone. The voice that always said to her 'I love you' in the casual way that other people said 'Good morning'. The timbre and tone as familiar as her own, so it was hard to adjust to the idea that this voice no longer wished to speak to her, no longer wished to wish her well.

One evening our route took us past the cemetery at the Old Deer Park and she told me about a funeral she had attended there the previous weekend; a photographer she had known some years before. They played Vivaldi on a tape at the grave. The last of the leaves falling with the pizzicato of the strings. 'I watched the widow weeping and envied her the certainty,' she said.

133

She thought constantly of the intimate things they had done together: Mike's hand on her stomach as a baby kicked; the raw tenderness of the first time they made love as each baby was a month or so old; tiny Lola cupped in his hands, a real little survivor, they all said so at the hospital, her bottom in his palm no bigger than an egg; the way, in the times when things were bad, he scratched her back in small circles until she fell asleep.

Now he was scratching Elizabeth's back and she was to get herself to sleep, though sometimes she didn't know how. His voice, when he finally picked up, on the telephone; she'd never find peace again: That's right! I've never been happy! Bang! Bang! The past as broken as a jigsaw that could no longer be assembled, too many of the pieces were bent or battered or missing: Were we happy or weren't we? It was a question she asked herself in various ways and one I couldn't answer.

I only met him once. He came round to pick up Lola to take her back to university. Lola was still getting her stuff and Morganna and I were shiny with thin sticks of rustic bread and a dish of fat olives that had been marinated in lemon and garlic. It was a delicious combination, the bread soaking up some of the olive oil. Morganna had a sensuous attitude to food, there was a best place to find everything delicious or sinful and always a treat with jasmine tea to drink before I set off for the boys: there were very sweet oranges cut into quarters with madeleines baked by a handsome Frenchman that she had run into that morning, wet almonds and butter tuiles that melted on the tongue.

When Mike arrived Morganna didn't invite him in, though she'd fussed about her hair a fair bit before he was due, coiling it and pinning it up here and there with the little silk flowers that she wore. I could see him on the doorstep while he waited for Lola to be ready, jigging a bit on the spot and throwing his balled-up scarf from hand to hand as though he was an athlete warming up, a bit of a player, a deluded fool with improbably matte brown hair. He looked like the sort of man who might sing at the London Palladium, though his trainers didn't quite go with the rest of it, the suit and striped silk tie. They were glaringly techno: thick soles and bi-coloured laces.

Sometimes I took Angus and Ivan round to Morganna's after school so that they could have a plonk on her piano. There was always chocolate cake and that bright green parrot of hers was easily encouraged to swear.

As the summer wore on the house was filling up with people: now when I was there I rarely had Morganna to myself, someone was always popping in or on the way out and she'd started to take in lodgers from the art school. Everyone wanted the rooms, she said; the house was right on the beach, so she got to pick.

But it wasn't until September when she came back from Scotland that everything really changed. The impending winter no longer cast such a frightening shadow. Her face was smooth in a way that it hadn't been in all the time I'd known her, as though it had been swept by a tide, and her eyes calm and completely clean of their usual clog of make-up. She was smiling, biting her lip just enough. Saying: 'I've set a date, Route 66.' She patted the driver's door of the camper van as though it were the shoulder of her horse – 'There's two months for us to knock me into shape' – and ran a finger along the chrome door handle. Then she hugged me as though we were already saying goodbye and a lump came to my throat.

I'd been at Marine Parade the night the call to Scotland came. My boys were happy enough thumping hornpipes on the piano and Simon was never at home in time to miss us anyway. She was doing her usual: sneaking around his bank account, sniffing at Elizabeth's Facebook, even Googling Elizabeth's friends: there was never anything much I could say to stop her. She tore her addict's eyes away from her computer, blazing.

'She's on holiday in the Highlands. Look, she's boasting about it here. Another holiday. I bet he's taken her to Kinlochie. I bet he's paying. Poor Lola, he won't even stump up for her health insurance premium now that she's eighteen and has dropped off his.'

Lola had been at Marine Parade earlier, still pallid and wheezy from a bronchitis. Morganna explained that it was because she had been so premature that she was prone to so many respiratory illnesses. Lola was beautiful in all the ways that made people tut about fashion models: tangles of hair appearing too vigorous for the light stem of her body, the stringy roots of her legs, slightly knock-kneed and junkie-pale.

'All her existing medical problems are still covered if he renews the policy. It doesn't make sense to let it lapse.' I had rarely seen Morganna so agitated, pulling at the rings and things around her neck until I thought the chain would break; I was glad that we weren't in a car with her at the wheel.

'He doesn't seem to understand that she's at university so she can't pay it herself.

'And I bet he's taken Elizabeth to Kinlochie!'

Ah yes, there he was in Kinlochie, happily cruising down the mountain path, whizzing really, taking the corners like Lance Armstrong, feeling good, he'd been working out at Elizabeth's gym, he could see the pleasing bulges of his thighs, a machine powering into the corners; Elizabeth quietly behind him, keeping up, just the whirr of the gears, not asking anything of him, her strong brown legs ending in bright white plimsolls over the pedals, pennants of hair flying, the super-brightness of her teeth, the almost uncontainably satiny thought that he'd be having sex with her later. He'd seen the Agent Provocateur bag in her luggage, heard the rustle of the tissue paper.

Probably it was a patch of gravel he hit. It could've been anything, there was always a lot of dry dung on the roads at that time of year, it was right out of the corner, maybe a stone, maybe a rut. He wasn't practised; hadn't really been mountain-biking much since the children grew up. Perhaps it was simply a niggled ridge of karma that sent his front wheel spinning.

Airlifted off the mountainside, no longer unconscious but still yabbering rubbish, taken by the throbbing helicopter along with his sobbing girlfriend to the mainland hospital where, even after his scans and a long sleep, the bang on his head was so severe that he could no longer remember who the hell this Elizabeth was.

Her tears puzzled him. He flinched from her hand like a child from its abductor. Wishing she'd hurry up. They kept asking him questions he couldn't answer, needing to know the name of his GP, his medical records. He couldn't remember a thing. 'When Morganna gets here, she'll tell you,' he said.

It was his private medical insurance that was covering it. A whole room to himself with adjoining bathroom. It was done up in minty green with oil paintings of unchallenging fields of corn on the walls. A television folded out from a bracket, the menu was bound in tooled leather.

He was propped up in bed, foolish and massively bruised with a bandage wrapped around his head like a turban. Elizabeth was sitting on a chair at his bedside, his obedient handmaiden, fingers knotted together in her lap. She stood up when Morganna was brought in. Morganna could see that Elizabeth's hands were shaking, she watched as she opened her mouth to speak but Mike's cries of, 'Morganna, my love. Thank God you're here,' silenced her. Elizabeth was shivering all over like a whippet. The nurse who had shown such kindness when she'd told Morganna where to go placed her hands around Elizabeth's thin cashmere wrists, looked into her eyes. 'Don't worry,' she said. 'This sometimes happens.' And Morganna felt like muttering, 'Turncoat.'

Elizabeth's voice was shaky when she found it. The caliph groaned and reached out his arms to Morganna, who found herself being pulled by him on to the bed, even treading on Elizabeth's toe as she was being swept up. She found herself in his arms, with her head on his chest, and she couldn't resist catching her breath there for a while, like coming home after being carried by a wave of nostalgia so powerful that it almost made her cry out. Elizabeth's words were lost to them both in the maelstrom but there was the sound of her voice shouting from the shore and then the slap of her shoes as she flounced from the room and along the corridor to the nurses' station.

'Looking for reinforcements,' said Morganna wickedly.

Morganna ran Mike a bath, testing it with her elbow in the way she'd tested it for their children. She promised to be gentle as she helped him from the bed.

He looked uncomfortable in the bath, a bit wary all hunched up like that, and stained by a great map of a bruise running from his ear through his shoulder and across his ribs. It wasn't a hot bath but beads of perspiration started breaking out all over his face beneath the bandage.

A second wave broke over her with even more force than the first. It came rushing up, taking her by surprise, dashing nostalgia on the rocks. Here he was, luxuriating in a bath because he'd banged his head. Their daughter was susceptible to lung problems; it came from being born twelve weeks too early. All his fault. She was twisting the flannel in her hands as she thought about the night that Lola emerged from between her legs mewling and helpless as a creature that had been freshly skinned. Mike seemed barely awake in the bath. The only person he ever paid for was Elizabeth, everyone else had been dropped.

'Will you give my back a scrub?' he murmured.

From what she'd found out, he was currently subsidising a vanity project, a record Elizabeth hoped to make, just herself with synthesizers and oboe.

Soapsuds gathered like scum around sparse tufts of hairs that sprouted randomly across his shoulders: she'd never noticed how hairy his back had become; she couldn't understand why Elizabeth wouldn't find him repulsive.

She had a sudden urge to sink her nails as hard as she could into that wet, sparsely forested skin. Lola brought on by the shock of some photographs she'd found nineteen years ago; so long ago now she'd almost managed to forget the name of the girl. Anyway, there had been others since to forget. Once she found a poem and a tube of KY jelly in his washbag and felt so tired that she didn't even mention it, only squeezed the jelly all over the poem, his toothbrush, his razor and the rest.

Mike had to keep his bandaged knees and arms bent above the line of the water; his arms rested along the rim of the bath and his deflated pectorals hung pale, reminding her of chicken fillets in their loose skin. She wrung the water from the flannel, trying to avoid thinking of it as his neck, and slapped it three times across her wrist, enough to sting. Mike didn't appear to notice, he was practically asleep, the weight of his head and the bandages making his chin sink to his chest.

A child couldn't escape a gestation cut short by twelve weeks without some sort of damage. Morganna's stomach turned at the sight of the hair in his armpits spread along the white rim of the hospital bath like the beards of mussels. Below, his scrotum bobbed slightly in the shallow water like giant figs. She imagined that this was how it would be to look at him through the eyes of Lucian Freud; the truth stripped bare: she could see the many blues and the purples of his skin, the places it was grey, all the varied shades of the abattoir. There was a tripe-pallor to it in the soft places too; she could see how his naked body would look when he died. There were parts of him she could see even further than that. Beneath the skin: the scar tissue bubbling up around his frozen shoulder, the stringy bits of contorted muscle beneath his naval where his hernia had been badly mended, the gathering fat closing in on itself in his arteries, like an oyster making a pearl but not beautiful.

It was as instant as falling in love, she said. She couldn't stop smiling. Flocks of birds were taking off from inside her head. She remembered a trip they took years before to California, the vibrating beds in the hotels. How good it felt when they turned themselves off. The pleasure and peace as the thrumming stopped. She assisted him from the bath, left him helplessly dripping on the mat; there had been a little blood seepage from the bandage at his head, she noticed. A small red star had spread on one side like a jewel.

She took a peach-coloured towel from the rail and wrapped it around him; an act of charity.

Elizabeth was at the door: 'Oh for God's sake, Morganna, stop . . .'

Elizabeth the one with the puffy eyes this time.

Morganna carried on patting her husband dry; his bandaged head was against her, his face pressed into her stomach like a child to its mother. Elizabeth hissed at her:

'You're sick.'

'Shshsh,' said Morganna cradling his head and looking at Elizabeth over the top of it.'

Elizabeth disappeared from the doorway. Morganna could hear the slight complaint of springs as she flung herself on to the hospital bed. It appeared the nurses were staying out of it after all. She could hear Elizabeth's sobbing, a childlike mewl that caused a drop of pity to fall onto the parched earth of her soul. She helped Mike into the gown that had been thoughtfully provided by the hospital and sat him on the softly chintzed chair that the Healthcare Trust had so kindly installed in the room.

'Christ, Morganna, my head is pounding,' he said. 'Do you think you could get that girl to stop crying?'

'I've got psittacosis! I've got psittacosis!' We could hear the parrot, the boys at its cage. Angus prompting: 'Say bugger! Say bugger!' Ivan's roaring laughter. Morganna stopped talking for a moment to lick her cigarette paper, to fold it down, to light it.

'Go on,' I said, ignoring my boys. Morganna looked to the door for a moment, exhaling in a way that always made me want to take up smoking.

'Oh Lord, he's not upstairs now, is he?' I said. 'You haven't taken him back, have you?'

Morganna threw back her head and laughed, her bracelets jingled as she wiped her eyes. We could hear Ivan and Angus pounding her piano again. The parrot still screeching. Morganna reached down and stroked her cat as it wound itself around her legs: the cat looked as keen to hear what happened next as I was myself. I glanced at my watch. It really was bad of me to still be here. Simon would be home already and I was going to make the boys late for bed. 'What happened?' I said.

Mike was sitting in the chair, not looking quite so dazed. She handed him a clipboard from her bag, and a pen. The steam had cleared from the room, everything had come into sharp focus: the sound of Elizabeth weeping, the buzz of the fan, the big red emergency cord that she could still see through the doorway hanging by the bath, her heart ticking like a clock.

On the clipboard, ready for him, was a policy for their daughter's health insurance; and that, she realised as he signed, was all she needed from him. Elizabeth was in the foetal position, she may even have been asleep. Morganna stopped for an instant, reached out a hand to the girl's cheek, was horrified when Elizabeth flinched. 'Everything will be all right,' she said.

Mike was leaning back a bit in the chair, his brow furrowed beneath the bandage as though with the effort of trying to catch more than glimpses of things that shimmered tantalisingly, minnowing in and out of his head.

'I'd better run if I'm to catch the post office in time with this,' said Morganna, tucking the policy safely into its envelope. Then she helped him up from the chair, and with Elizabeth's assistance, delivered him like an unwanted gift, or something she'd bought by mistake in the wrong size, back to his bed.

At Arka Pana

It was really a little soon for a whole weekend away but when he called, Claudine found herself agreeing to go. His mother was ill: 'I'd like her to meet you.' So ill: 'It has to be now.' When they got to Krakow, he said, they would eat *pierogi*, delicious apparently, and he would take her to a church of river stones that was shaped like the Ark.

Claudine hadn't a clue what she should wear to meet this mother. She hoped the poor woman wouldn't die from shock when he announced their news. From what he'd told her so far she was a bit of a termagant, with a habit of throwing shoes when cross. Probably best to cover her tattoo. The butterfly at her ankle flapped its wings as she flexed her foot. She folded a couple of T-shirts, pants, socks, jeans, everyday things, put them on top of her trainers in the bag, rummaging through the wardrobe, through all the carefree clothes jammed on the hangers.

He wants her to meet his mother. Only a week ago the touch of his arm tucked through hers had still felt quite forward: lunch in London, a walk through Hyde Park, he was formal, careful not to rush things, even stopping to admire the bright new leaves uncurling from their buds. But impossible to deny that there was something there. Phone calls followed, very long ones, and a night last week when they'd got sozzled and sentimental at a restaurant in Marine Parade. He'd told her of his childhood in Krakow; she'd told him of hers by the sea.

That night they stayed out late and discovered a shared passion for chocolate cherry brandies, walking in the rain and Pablo Neruda's sea poems. By the time they got back to her house, they were soaked through and she felt like she'd known him for ever. They both preferred long baths to short showers, coffee to tea and always remembered their dreams. He could quote great chunks of her favourite poetry. They chatted for over an hour just standing at the front gate, despite the rain which showed no sign of stopping, splashing on the stones of the front path, dripping from their hair.

'You know,' she said. 'You can stay.' She was sure her mum wouldn't mind; at least she hoped she wouldn't.

He'd held her at arm's length the better to look her full in the face: lucky, he said, that he had a driver booked from the station because it was tempting, given the hour, but he really didn't think he was ready to come face to face with her mother. It had been a lovely sort of rain, an April shower, just falling neatly, making halos of every street light, no wind or bluster but his hair was plastered to his forehead, his lashes spiked. He'd been holding his coat like a shelter over both of their heads, but hers mainly. It was almost unnerving how handsome he seemed to her at that moment.

'Mum!' Pale yellow sunshine streamed in through her thin bedroom curtains. She shouted to Aurelia through her open bedroom door.

'Do you have my passport?' The whole landing reeked of Aurelia's most expensive bath foam.

Claudine stumbled about, gathering things from the drawers of her dressing table. Rifling for the second time through her wardrobe made her stamp her foot and she held out two dresses on hangers before her, neither of them perfect.

'Do you really think I'll need something smart?' she shouted again through the door but still there wasn't an answer, just another bout of rumbling from the hot water pipes.

The newer of the two dresses was black crochet, halter-necked, tight across the hips, possibly a bit too body-skimming to be comfortable. The one she usually wore for smart occasions was still her favourite: vintage from eBay, yellow with a full skirt and a belt of embroidered daisies. She shook the hangers and wondered about ironing. Would the daisies look a bit childish if she was meeting his friends? 'We'll probably all get drunk and moan about the communist times,' he'd said. 'You make it sound irresistible,' she'd replied, laughing.

She looked from the black dress to the pastel flounces. She wouldn't be able to fit them both in if she was to pack her Doc Martens. He'd specified hand luggage when he called.

'Mum,' she tried again, attempting to keep the whininess from her voice.

Aurelia emerged from her steamy chamber smelling of unguents, wrapped in a towel, hair in a turban. She was a scalded pink, as though she'd had a good old scrub at herself with the loofah. Claudine raised an eyebrow and sniffed ostentatiously at the air.

'I ought to look my best, don't you think?' Aurelia said with only a slight smile.

In her room Aurelia buttoned a grey cashmere cardigan over her black bra with its acres of black lace and Claudine regretted that she hadn't inherited breasts like her mother's. She wandered over and put her hand to Aurelia's shoulder and Aurelia reached up and ruffled Claudine's hair. 'Are you going to be OK?' she said.

'It feels peculiar,' Claudine replied. 'Going all that way to meet his mother, I mean . . .'

Aurelia pulled the top of the cardigan together and pinned her moonstone brooch in place.

'. . . I wish you were coming.' Claudine cringed at herself. She sounded about six years old.

Aurelia flicked at her damp hair and the hairdryer drowned out anything else that Claudine might have wanted to say. Aurelia's hair always took an age to dry: wavy and dark and very thick. Claudine raked her hands through her own mop, making it stand up like Bart Simpson's, watching herself in the mirror above Aurelia's head and tilting her chin. She had her mother's mouth: big lips and ever so slightly crooked teeth; she looked from Aurelia to herself. But she had her father's curls, his eyes, his double lashes, no doubt about that. The buzz of the hairdryer became intolerable and she wandered back to her packing. There'd be time for talking later. She almost couldn't bear the wait for him to arrive.

It seemed just as bad for Aurelia too. Claudine had never known her mother so distracted. It had gone on all day yesterday: a fuss about a coffee pot; a bustle about the flowers, yellow tulips now artfully arranged in crystal bowls downstairs; some sort of hassle with the Hoover. Even the piano had been tuned. Its black case had been polished to an obsidian shine, and it presided over the room with a certain cold majesty that gave Claudine nightmares. She had a vision of Aurelia launching herself at its keys and playing the Hallelujah chorus when he arrived.

Claudine couldn't remember a time when her mother hadn't been hammering at the piano for hours every day; even worse were her students. She used to think of other people's houses as sanctuaries, as piano-free havens where reading and thinking were occasionally accompanied only by the gentle buzz of a television. Here, the gleaming piano took up half the living room and most of the oxygen. A carnivorous old thing, it had teeth rather than keys and a lid just right for trapping little fingers.

The check-in time for Krakow was very early so it was brief when it happened. He was exactly on time: the clock had just finished chiming. Spring sunshine flashed through the front door. Aurelia's shoulders stiffened, Claudine saw her take a deep breath as she opened it wider. Leszek was wearing a hat, a black felt one, which he lifted, making his greeting over-formal, his hair flattened on top.

Aurelia stood aside to let him in and he bent to kiss her cheek.

The hall seemed crowded by the three of them and Claudine was minutely aware of the ticking of the clock through the wall. He reached an arm to her, through air that was thick with unknown things. 'Beautiful girl,' he said, kissing her forehead, the briefest of hugs: he'd been smoking; she could smell it in the wool of his jacket. Then back to kiss Aurelia's cheek again, or maybe even to hug her too, but she was stiff as a bottle and all at once it occurred to Claudine that this meeting might not be quite the euphoric thing she wished it to be. Leszek handed her a bottle of champagne that was cold but needed to be chilled.

'I know it's early for drinking alcohol but I think we should celebrate,' he said, looking nervously to Aurelia, as though seeking her permission. His wool jacket was a black pea coat, it suited him, went well with the black felt hat. Aurelia gestured to the sitting room, and Claudine almost stamped her foot with irritation that the first thing he did was to fawn over the piano.

The piano was perfectly in tune, almost smugly so. Leszek couldn't resist lifting the lid and running his fingers over a couple of keys. 'Nice,' he said.

It had been relentlessly brought to this state of refined equal temperament by the local tuner, Richard, a noticeably younger and more tousled specimen than the regular London man.

Aurelia had been in Hamburg the first time the London tuner hadn't made it so Claudine had dealt with everything. The new guy was OK, she'd said. This time, however, they'd barely exchanged a word on the doorstep before Aurelia, coming down, caught sight of him standing there and flew the last of the stairs.

'Ricky? Richard!' she exclaimed and his face went the colour of salami. 'So many years since I've seen you!

'I hadn't heard word of you since the Guild. And now here you are!' He smiled slightly nervously at her. 'I never had another student who played the Haydn quite as you did . . . I expected to find a recording by you one of these days.' Richard hung his head as he fiddled with his roll of tuning tools. 'Ah well,' he said. 'In another life maybe.' Claudine excused herself from her mother's excruciating lack of tact. She always hated the racket of the piano being tuned, the dinging of the notes, the constant comparison, the trills to nowhere and back.

Claudine crammed the champagne bottle into the freezer. She watched from the doorway as Leszek went from the piano to the sofa. It was a strange sight: him perched on the edge of their sofa, turning his hat in his hands.

Aurelia was staring at him with her arms crossed over her chest and he seemed to be talking to the floor.

'It must've been odd seeing Rick again,' he was saying.

'He says he's given up all performing. He had such talent!' Aurelia wandered over to the window; only at the word 'talent' did she turn to Leszek.

Leszek looked stranded, the green leather sofa an island surrounded by uncertain tides. 'Yes, I can imagine,' he said, coughing into his fist.

'He was the best in his year . . .' she said. 'Well, apart from you, I suppose.'

The piano tuner had at least given them something to talk about, Claudine thought bitterly, looking from one to the other: at Leszek, so fascinated by his own thumbs playing again at the brim on his hat; at Aurelia's evasive eyes.

'Talented but no confidence. He was never going to be any good,' Leszek said.

'His Haydn Fantasia in C was about as lovely as I've ever heard it played,' she countered.

'Yes, but what was the use? Remember the Wigmore Hall?'

Aurelia grimaced. 'Poor Ricky, what a time for stage fright.'

'Ah yes, poor Rick,' he agreed.

Claudine couldn't believe how bored they were making her feel with this tragedy. She might as well have not been in the room.

Leszek coughed and Aurelia seemed to suddenly remember, almost with a jolt, that she actually had a daughter, and walked to where she was slouching in the doorway. She cupped a hand to her cheek.

'Richard was always very jealous of Leszek,' she explained, and then she smiled across at Leszek in the way that Claudine had always hoped she would.

'Your father, I mean.' She moved her hand up to her own face, covering her eyes.

'Your father.' Leszek echoed her and coughed again, almost theatrically.

Aurelia jumped. 'Anyone want anything? A glass of orange juice? Buck's Fizz?'

Leszek had been quiet all the way to Gatwick. Claudine looked at him sideways a couple of times, mainly trying to decide in which ways his profile resembled her own; then when he still wasn't speaking, she put her feet on the dash and had a quick rally of texts back and forth with her friend Laura.

'Would you have recognised her?' she asked him when she could stand his silence no longer. 'Has she changed?'

Leszek only shrugged. Claudine wondered why she'd agreed to this trip. She was missing two pretty good parties on Saturday night; Laura had texted that she had a new leather jacket.

Even on the flight he still didn't want to talk: 'To tell you the truth, I feel quite angry with your mother', was all he said when she questioned him about his silence. 'Seventeen years is a long time to keep a secret.'

They drank Bloody Marys and then he asked if she'd mind if he read his newspaper? She said she didn't, and it could have been worse but she noticed him glancing at her a couple of times, and then he noticed her noticing and smiled, which made her feel better.

As they were landing in Krakow he shared what his mother's doctor had told him on the phone. 'We must be prepared for the worst,' he said, and Claudine understood then that his silence on this journey might have little to do with her. She tried to imagine his pain. It was odd, she thought, the way things had turned out: he was losing a parent just as she was gaining one.

Everything had gone very smoothly; the hire car smelled not unpleasantly of mandarin oranges. It wasn't like travelling with Aurelia where stuff got lost on the luggage carousel.

They were still early for the hospital so they stopped for *pierogi* in the bright sunlight of Rynek Square, where the Easter market was spilling across the cobbles in a profusion of stalls and baskets and painted eggs and bright chrysanthemums. The *pierogi* came on paper plates and they perched to eat them at a wooden table with an hour to kill.

'I've never met a grandmother before,' she said. The *pierogi* was quite chewy for a dumpling, with a filling of greasy cheese.

'That's right.' He nodded his head, chewing slowly, as though vaguely recalling an arcane fact. 'I remember now. Rae was brought up only by her father, you wouldn't have a grandmother on her side.'

Claudine liked that he called Aurelia 'Rae', but still she'd have preferred that Aurelia's family circumstances were indelibly engraved on his heart.

'I think she was very young when she lost her mother, am I right?' he said.

'How well did you actually know her?' Claudine hadn't meant to sound sharp, nor spill her coffee. 'She told me you lived together.'

Leszek put his hand beneath the brim of his hat to cover his brow. 'We did live together', and left it there while he told her how it felt to be lost in music and she dabbed at the puddle of coffee with a napkin. 'Even if Snow White and the Seven Dwarfs had moved in I'm not sure I would have noticed—'

'Did you really not know she was pregnant? Is that the truth?' Claudine interrupted him.

'. . . When I wasn't playing I was imagining the music I would play.' He took another bite of his *pierogi*. He was a great one for talking with his mouth full.

'You can't understand what it was like: I had finished all the studying I would ever do: the exams, the constant assessments, the marks from one to five for my playing from the steel-faced judges in room number seven.' Here he grimaced at his fingers, as though he'd suddenly discovered warts.

He shook his hands free of their afflictions, jumping up from his seat. 'I had already been taught by two great masters here in Poland. The iron curtain had lifted and I was free.' Leszek swung his arms out wide, making a woman step sideways.

He raised his hat to the woman, an all too handsome apology. The woman smiled.

'I wanted to play everything,' he said, pulling her hands and lifting her to her feet, practically jigging on the spot.

'I wanted to write music and play music from Bach to The Beatles and back again. I wanted to write down my own music. But before you write it down it has to live in your head, the dynamics, the articulation, it all needs to be there before you touch a key of the piano.'

'Oh God, now you're behaving like my mother,' groaned Claudine, plonking herself down again. 'I can't stand the piano.'

She wiped her greasy fingers on another napkin and screwed it into a twist with the paper plate. She aimed and missed the bin and Leszek leapt to pick it up before she had a chance to retrieve it herself.

'Going to tell me off for dropping litter now, are you, Dad?' she said, the strange heat of the word as it left her mouth, and the smile that it brought to his, making her suddenly furious.

He pointed across the cobbles to a stall where wicker baskets were filled with tall displays of dried grasses and flowers.

'I was twenty-three years old when you were born,' he said. 'I was already in New York.' He shrugged a couple of times and pointed again to the stall.

'Look,' he said, pulling her across the street, as easily as a man changing channels on the television. 'We always had these in our house at Easter. Why don't we get Aurelia a traditional Easter palm? Do you think she'd like that? Is it her sort of thing?'

Claudine gulped; the grease from the *pierogi* was still in her mouth. She hoped she wasn't about to cry as he led her through the avenues of painted eggs and elaborate handicrafts, the flowers and the carvings, the baskets and yet more painted eggs and the rabbits and the chickens made from wicker and feathers and fluff.

Puppets had nightmarish faces: even the ones of little boys and girls in traditional dress had the bulging eyes of constant strangulation.

'Peculiar for a puppet state, don't you think?' he said as a busking violinist shook his hat at them and the wings of the pigeons flapped so close that a shiver ran down the back of her neck. 'We already had such a tradition of puppetry.'

He pointed to the statue of Adam Mickiewicz raised high on its plinth at the opposite end of the square: 'Our greatest bard and philanderer,' he said, and she thought she might as well be walking around with a tour guide for all the difference it made.

Her phone was like an itch in her pocket. She wondered who Laura would get off with at the party. She hoped Laura's new leather jacket wasn't too much like her own. Claudine couldn't bear it when her friends started copying her look.

No time to stop and text though. Leszek was steering her towards a stall of fancy iced cakes. '*Mazurek*,' he said. 'Very traditional.' Leszek chose a large ginger one for his mother, covered in lurid green and red cherries with the word 'Hallelujah' in waves of white icing.

She was thinking what a shame it was that language wasn't genetic. If she'd been born with the ability to speak Polish she'd be able to understand what he was saying to everyone, though it didn't sound such a pretty language. She heard her name in the middle of something and interrupted him while he was paying for the cake.

'This cake is for your mother?' she said.

'Yes, your grandmother.'

'If she's just had major surgery, will she want to eat cake like that?'

He laughed. 'You'll see. She's strong as an ox. A Polish ox. None stronger.'

Claudine was right about the cake. The bountiful gingerbread with its glossy fruit and fat white 'Hallelujah' did nothing but highlight the frailty of the old woman propped in the hospital bed amidst the wires and the tubes. '*Matka*,' he said and the tears bulged and slid from his eyes and he did nothing to wipe them away. He sat on the only chair by her bedside, crying silently, cradling her tiny yellow hand. '*Matka*.'

Claudine couldn't believe that anyone could be that shade of the paintbox. She could feel her own bile and stomach juices. The hospital smelled of old school dinners. Leszek seemed to have forgotten her existence. She hovered, uneasily shifting her weight from foot to foot behind him. Her grandmother's breathing was shale at the shore, her tongue a dehydrated cockle. The whites of her eyes were as jaundiced as her face. She didn't seem particularly aware that her son was at her bedside. Claudine had never seen anyone die: it was grotesque.

She was shaky but Leszek needed to sleep when they got back to the hotel so there was nothing he could do to comfort her. He apologised for leaving her alone. 'I am too sad to stay awake,' he said, shrugging. Then, hours later, when he finally revived from his nap, they were straightaway on the drive across town, friends to see, and much to tell about the monuments they passed on the way. Leszek's inner tour guide had made a good recovery: even his hair looked springier and he'd had a shave. He had an apricot-coloured scarf knotted at his neck to break up the black, a good choice.

Claudine felt only worse for the solitude: while he'd napped or cried or shaved, or whatever it was he'd been doing for the last three hours, she'd managed only to pick spots, row with her mother on the telephone and watch herself cry in the hotel room mirror.

'He was too wrapped up in his music. There wouldn't have been any point in telling him . . .' Aurelia still defended her decision. 'I was so much older. I didn't want to tie him down.'

'But it might've been nice for me.' Claudine had picked so hard at her chin that a small spot of blood appeared, the telephone wedged to her shoulder.

'As soon as I saw you all fat and pink I knew that I wanted you to be all mine.' This was the bit that Claudine had heard a million times before and she took the phone from her ear, ready to cut the line.

'As I held you in my arms the waves of love were so strong . . .' Aurelia had been saying. By the time Leszek emerged from his room, ready to go out, with his hands tucked into the pockets of his black pea coat and the bright scarf, Claudine was already regretting that she'd put the phone down.

Leszek's hands tapped along on the steering wheel to a tune in his head. She watched him chew his lip and tried to imagine him in the school hall with all the other parents, but none of the other fathers looked like a brooding hero and the thought of him being there made her laugh out loud.

They were passing some particularly splendid buildings, dramatically lit with spotlights, and Leszek resumed his educational spiel: the town hall, the Mongol hordes, the kings at Wassel Hill, ignoring her sputtering laughter.

'Tomorrow, before we visit *Matka* in the hospital, I will take you to the town I was from. To where *Matka* has lived all her life,' he said. 'Nowa Huta, it's quite famous. I think you'll find the architecture astonishing.'

Yeah, like hell, she thought. She wondered how much time they had left before he would have to take himself back to New York. She wondered what arrangements they'd make to stay in touch. He gestured to some more gracious buildings of golden stone.

'And imagine all this splendour and just down the road Auschwitz,' he said. Claudine nodded wearily. Why was it that everyone always felt such an urge to educate her?

They passed a man on a unicycle. He was wearing a business suit and carrying a polythene shopping bag in each hand. Claudine sank down in her seat, wondering if the lacy tights worked with her Doc Martens, and remembering driving through a town rather like this one, with lots of old stone and history, on a holiday when she was younger.

It was somewhere in Italy, maybe Naples. She'd been touring with her friend and her friend's father for long enough to lose interest in place names. She was missing her mother and suspected she'd been brought along, a bit like a frisbee, as holiday entertainment for the friend.

Every time her friend's father had to brake, even a little bit, Claudine would endure the sight of his arm shooting out to the side to protect his daughter, though the front seats were the ones with seatbelts. He would ruffle her hair or pinch her lightly on the cheek, a secret smile would pass between them before he put both hands back to the wheel. All holiday long Claudine had observed this little ritual from the rear seat of the car. It was noisy and hot and they'd had to drive with the windows open, which meant she couldn't ever hear their conversation in the front.

'Tomorrow I'll show you the church my mother helped to build,' Leszek was saying. 'She took a rock from the river and carried it in her arms like a huge stone baby.'

Claudine's brief fury melted away as she remembered how sad he must be.

'It's called the People's Ark, you'll see why tomorrow. Everyone brought the stones, on their horses, in carts; all two million stones brought by the people. Mainly it was a symbolic act,' he told her. 'The Pope sent a stone from St Peter's tomb and a crystal from the moon was sent by the Apollo 11 mission.'

Claudine noticed as he leaned over to the glove compartment for his glasses that although his hair was springy as her own, it was slightly thinning, so that the gap between the curls was wider than would be expected at the top of his head.

'The lunar crystal's been set in the tabernacle,' he told her.

All he ever did was talk at her like a tourist brochure, ignoring that there were plenty of things she wanted him to say, none of them to do with the history of a town or its buildings. She was being driven mad by Laura's texts: the parties she was missing. It sounded like Laura's leather jacket was identical to her own. She ought to call her mother back, she thought; but then he was parking and there wasn't time.

Leszek's friends lived on the top floor of a modernist block of glass and red-painted metal. The lift was mirrored, like in a department store. Claudine stole a look as they went up, not speaking. She could see the resemblance, probably anyone could: something about the slope of the shoulders, the way they were standing. In the face, the thick brows: the same shape exactly as her own, the dense dark eyelashes, certainly those.

Inside the apartment there was metal in the places you'd expect to see wood, black shiny furniture, stark walls of bare brick. She offered silent thanks to Aurelia for suggesting she pack the black dress, she'd have felt like Fairy Daffodil dressed in the yellow while eight of Leszek's friends just stared at her as though she'd burst out of a cake.

'Leszek's daughter!' they exclaimed. And then everyone laughed a little too loudly for a little too long, including Claudine. For a moment she felt like she'd landed in the middle of a group hallucination. They stared at her, still no one moved from the semi circle, trendy mourners in shades of crow, the women especially very thin, and then one of them, Elzbieta, clapped her hands and the others did too. One of the men wolf-whistled through the gap in his teeth.

'Swavjik is my oldest friend,' Leszek said, introducing her to the whistler, who wore a fine-knit black cardigan that almost reached his knees and a smile as wide as a slice of melon.

'Wow, Leszek, what a beautiful daughter.'

Before her face grew too hot, Malgosha, tall in a pin-striped man's suit, swooped to her rescue, taking Claudine by the elbow and steering her towards a jug of margarita and a tray of glasses. She poured from the jug. 'So, you tell me all about your mother,' she said, holding up a tumbler that was misted with ice. 'She must have been one strong woman!'

'What do you mean, *strong*?' said Claudine, accepting the glass and hoping that margarita was one of the drinks that she liked.

'Secret for seventeen years!' said Malgosha, her smile a gash of newly-applied lipstick. 'If I had Leszek's baby I think I'd shout it from every rooftop!' Claudine raised her glass and chinked it to Malgosha's. She needed this margarita, whatever it was.

'Best thing at the time,' Aurelia had said on the phone. Yeah, she thought. Best for who exactly? The drink was strong. One thing was proving to be true: life around Leszek was awash with alcohol.

Dinner was red wine with pasta and sausages and then there was sweet wine with a chocolate tart and some sour cherries. Despite the rivers of booze everyone managed well in English, though occasionally the table got thumped and then there'd be a loose stream of Polish, all of them talking at once.

When Leszek asked Swavjik if he'd roll a joint Claudine shivered on the edge of outrage; what was she supposed to do if they passed it to her? Watching it being rolled reminded her of the parties she was missing. She started to feel almost panicky at the thought of the joint.

She was probably just as out of it as she would've been on this Saturday night on her home turf but instead of dancing she was struggling to follow a conversation about an orchestra, stuck on a wire chair between Leszek and his doleful friend Bazyl, a man with black-rimmed glasses and the looks of a spy. She tuned in and out of the debate about the orchestra. Swavjik's flat was like something out of a magazine at the dentist: the table of thick black glass, everything rattling about when it got thumped, lots of chrome, strange globes of light hanging from chains overhead like giant light bulbs suspended from industrial steel joists. The chairs were close relations to shopping trolleys and, across the room, with its lid suggestively open, Swavjik's inevitable piano loomed like an elephant.

Leszek settled his back against his chair, knees to the table, and she watched him bring Swavjik's skinny joint to his lips, watched it glow as he took a pull and waited, holding her own breath, for his long exhalation. For some reason she was reminded of a hot summer's day, years before; a picnic by a river in Dorset, annoying little flies and jam sandwiches, Aurelia and the other grown-ups giggling and stripping off their T-shirts and jeans to go skinny-dipping from the bank.

He took another tug on the joint, narrowing his eyes. Claudine tried to remember if any of her friends' fathers took drugs in front of their children. She thought maybe Laura's once did. He exhaled again and spared her the embarrassment by passing it straight back to Swavjik before exploding in coughs.

In Dorset the grown-ups slipping and sliding down the bank, swinging breasts, white bums, daring each other to make the first splash. She'd never seen a penis before and now there were three just bobbing around. Aurelia whooping and laughing along with everyone else, the pelts of fur, the dancing penises, her burning shame as she sat with the other children with the jam sandwiches on the grass.

Talk had turned rather predictably to music: Leszek promised he'd play. Malgosha told him about a composer she was working with. 'A very idiosyncratic project,' she said and everyone seemed to find it interesting. They were speaking slowly, stumbling for words of imperfect English because she was there. 'Id-io-syn-cratic.' Malgosha looked pleased with herself. 'Please feel free to just carry on between yourselves in your own language' – that's what Claudine thought she should've said. Leszek was telling Swavjik something about some work he was doing with a rock band. He seemed to have forgotten she existed.

Swavjik got overheated about the avant-garde turn that Leszek's career had taken: 'I suppose we forgive that he gave up playing the greatest music ever written,' he said, banging the table, and Claudine wondered if Leszek made a habit of giving things up. Her head was starting to spin. 'He was putting things inside the piano to see how they would sound. Always. Pencil cases, cloths, even his shoes.'

Malgosha joined in. 'He was mad,' she said. 'He and Swav never stopped practising. They were competing to see who could practise the longest. Seven hours sometimes. Both mad!'

It probably would have been better if she'd allowed herself to be sick at Swavjik's; Claudine's pounding head was proof enough. Swavjik's place had been at sea the whole time Leszek played the piano, while she slumped in a chair of black leather straps, and he'd played for what felt like a year. She didn't know what was worse: the sound of last night's piano spinning around the echoing flat with the bright globes hanging from the rafters, or the piped music that was now burrowing into her brain in the breakfast lounge of the hotel. The sight of Leszek's scrambled eggs made her mouth sour. He poured her a glass of water, popped a couple of paracetamol from their foil and passed them across the table to her along with a Danish pastry that he'd carefully wrapped in a napkin to put in her pocket for later.

'Ready to see Nowa Huta?' he said, shaking the hire car keys, and the rattling made her wince.

They parked beside a green kiosk, ALKO HOLE, its name biliously in red on the green boards.

'Keep your phone out of sight,' he said. 'It can be a bit dodgy in this part.' A sad wind blew up the street, a bus belched by looking a little rusty. Nowa Huta appeared to have been made entirely out of Lego. They'd driven for an hour through its thoroughfares, unwavering blocks of it, street after street. 'Stalin's dream,' Leszek, her irrepressible tour guide, had explained. Grey Lego. Straight roads and tall poplars spaced as evenly as soldiers. Row upon row of concrete uniformity, slotted together beneath a wishy-washy sky. 'Uncle Joe's workers' paradise, some of these have almost five hundred apartments,' Leszek said, gesturing skywards at towering blocks like human filing cabinets.

His beloved Arka Pana church now rose across the street like a great hulk beached beside the pavement. 'The people's ark.' He threw open both arms as though bowing to a great beauty.

The concrete walkways didn't look much like Mount Ararat as the traffic streamed relentlessly by. The church itself was a great modern lump of a thing, reddish brown and flat on top. From where they waited to cross, it looked like it might have been pebble-dashed. It could have been a trendy library in a development town.

'The state would not give an ounce of steel for this church. The people had to do it all themselves. Even the concrete was mixed with shovels, they wouldn't even lend the big machinery.'

Its windows were cut in at odd angles and its walls bulged outwards. A huge cross rose from the roof like a mast with a gold crown where the pennant would fly.

'Not what the Soviets wanted to see being built in their Godless model city,' he said.

Claudine wished they had never come to Poland. It seemed so long ago that they had walked together along the shore in the rain, though it had been only days. It was simple then. He'd asked her to tell him a happy memory for every year of her life that he'd missed. Now he gestured at the church: 'Thousands of people used to gather and prayers were said for Poland to be free from oppression.'

Claudine stifled a yawn. A dog was barking high up on

a balcony. It was tied up and between barks they could hear its chain rattling against the bars. Two boys in knee-length parkas scuffed past them on the scrubby patch of green. They turned to double take Claudine, the spottiest one pretended to trip. She wondered if Leszek might take her hand as they crossed the road. He'd held her hand almost naturally when they'd walked along by the sea. They'd swung their arms together. She'd told him that her earliest memory wasn't a happy one: it concerned the brake failing on her pushchair. 'It sounds like that scene from *The Battleship Potemkin*,' he said, shuddering. 'Only tell me happy things. Please don't make me sad.'

So she'd obliged with stories of Indian tents and birthday cakes and swimming races and scenes remembered more from watching videos of happy occasions than from the happy occasions themselves. She'd told him about the first time she saw snow and the day that Aurelia unscrewed the stabilisers from her bike.

Arka Pana loomed over them; what had looked like pebble-dash from across the road was actually millions of large smooth river stones, set into its walls. An abstract glass panel shaped like a sail hung over the door.

'When they weren't allowed to have a church, thousands used to come to this very spot to hear midnight Mass under the stars,' he said after they'd dodged the traffic and slipped through the glass doors, his hand on her elbow to guide her.

It was a little cool inside, and muted: silent as a well. She noticed how the highest panels of glass were set in a long curve, like rigging. 'My mother used to bring me to mass when it was just an open field. I remember it was freezing cold.'

Claudine looked around, at the smooth grey concrete flanks of the walls, at the modern art that was hung there. From the side a muscular bronze Jesus Christ appeared to be flying rather than being crucified. He was leaping, balletic, though his arms and legs were in the crucifixion pose: toes pointed, long sinewy arms thrown back.

'Suffering and redemption,' Leszek said, pointing to the Christ. 'During the communist times this church offered the people a chance to meet and to speak freely.'

The church was empty, apart from two women in overalls sweeping the floor. Leszek and Claudine sat at the end of a pew made of heavily varnished pale wood, like the desks in a Victorian school. She wasn't surprised to see him bow his head.

She knew he needed to pray hard and tried to turn her own thoughts to her grandmother in the hospital; she should feel something other than dread. They would be visiting *Matka* again when they left the church, once Leszek had done with speaking to this God. Claudine wondered if he might have tried to share his God with her if he'd been around; she'd only got a rather languid agnostic pose to thank Aurelia for. It might have been nice to have a God. She touched the mole above her lip on the left side of her face. '*Babcia*', as Leszek had said she must call her, *Babcia* had a mole, the same size, in the same position only hers sprouted a few thick white hairs.

'*Matka*, this is your granddaughter,' he had said in gentle Polish and Claudine wasn't sure if her tears were for her grandmother or for herself. Too late, *Babcia*. It was like looking at a husk. She'd never know her now. She wished Leszek could have found her sooner. That whoever had sent the anonymous letter to him in New York had done so earlier.

At last he lifted his head from his hands. It was so quiet in the Ark that she could hear the drop of water falling into the font.

'Can we speak?' she said into her hands.

'Yes,' he said, putting his palm to the back of her head, so she'd look at him. 'I do want to talk. I can see you are troubled. Tell me, what do you want to know?'

The irony of their surroundings wasn't lost on her. Here they were in a sacred space, a public place, and yet it felt like the right place to finally demand the truth. They both leaned their elbows on the back of the pew in front.

'You didn't move to New York until three months before I was born,' she said. 'Surely someone must have noticed that she was pregnant? I've worked out the timing. Did you really have no idea?'

'All my dreams were about music, melodies, harmonies, about the sounds I would get out of the piano.' He had no apologies to make.

'You went away. She didn't even have a number for you . . .'

'She could have got it. Seventeen years is a long time to keep a secret.'

'You were twenty-three. Would you have demanded your share of me?' Claudine almost giggled at the thought of it, and then went silent. She could feel the buzz of a message on her phone in her pocket but she ignored it.

'What were you doing when I was born?' she added when he still didn't reply. Two nuns had come into the church. She could hear the small rustlings of their habits as they moved around the flowers and the candles.

After a moment where it seemed he couldn't hold her gaze he took a deep breath, putting his hat on his head and then pulling it off again.

'I was still on tour with the guys, all that year,' he said. 'We went to South America, Cuba, met Ry Cooder, it's the best I ever played.' He flexed his fingers and looked at them sadly.

'Would you have had me for half the holidays, that sort of thing?' Claudine couldn't stop now that she'd started.

She turned to look again at Christ, at his ecstatic leap, the blocks of painted concrete behind him only hinting at a crucifixion, at his concentration-camp ribcage and a crown of thorns that looked more like barbed wire.

His leaping from his bonds made her bold: 'Would you have come back to her for my sake if you had known that she was pregnant?' He looked terribly sad then. She noticed the clanging of the bells. They'd been ringing for quite a while, they echoed in her ears. 'It's OK,' she said. 'You don't have to lie.'

'I'd heard the rumours, could do the maths,' he said. 'People called, at first.' He too looked up at the Christ, who had his head turned to the bluish light flooding through the slice of window: a noble profile with a goatee beard and an aquiline nose.

'All my life, all I've ever wanted to do is to play my own music. I was in the Academy in Gdansk from when I was seven. Practise, practise, practise. My mother working her whole life to make that possible. Physical work, she had calluses on her hands sometimes. Rubbed raw.

172

'When I was home I'd come with her to this church that she'd helped to build. I remember a ZOMO militiaman hitting her across the shoulders with a baton, her arms, her back, over and over again as I tried to pull her away. She always wanted to give as good as she got. There was always fighting. These ZOMO people were a bit out of their brains, like your football hooligans.

'If there was a riot then there was tear gas and we had to run and crowd into the apartments nearby where we could put the cream on our eyes. One time I remember they fired fluorescent dye with the water from the tanks and we were marked for days afterwards and after dusk the UV patrols with their powerful reflectors, the dye impossible to wash out of our clothes, always waiting to be beaten up. Do you understand?' he said.

'I prayed and prayed that I would be allowed one day to have a life playing my own music, that's all I wanted. Where's the harm in music? I was sick of feeling frightened. That life had just started for me when I knew your mother; I met her at the Guild when I'd only just arrived. I always thought she'd have no trouble meeting somebody else. I was already heading for New York even before I lived with her.'

He looked almost out of breath when he'd finished speaking. 'Come on,' he said, taking her arm. 'Let's get out of here.'

She imagined him always running: London, America, South America, Cuba. It was bad enough when Aurelia had to go away to play in this city or that festival but there had always been careful arrangements.

'Oh God,' she said. 'If you'd been around I'd have been orphaned twice-over by the piano.'

Usually she'd been sent to stay next door. The daughter, Lottie, who was pale and these days ate nothing but Quark, always had everything that Claudine wanted. The father owned a toy shop and sometimes Lottie didn't even bother to get the things out of their boxes. 'When people get what they want they haven't got a clue what to do with it,' Aurelia said.

Leszek opened the door to the pavement. 'So few young people come to the church now,' he said as they went out of the Ark.

'After all that fighting. Molotov cocktails and beatings. Now we don't like to be constrained by anything, not even religion.'

They stood together on the wall at the top of the steps outside, watching the people gather. It had started to spot with rain. 'Hey, I'm very glad you're in the world,' he said, tipping her under the chin, and then both their phones rang at once and they bent away from each other to answer.

The bells were making it difficult. The hospital was calling him, 'Oh, oh, oh, oh no . . .' he said when he heard the news. Laura was on the end of hers, party post-mortem, non-stop: everyone got hammered. Crap band. Her jacket got nicked. A bit of a whoopsie: she'd take the morning after pill. The people flowed past, parting like a river around the man and the girl standing apart from each other on the path talking into their mobile phones.

Ivan Knows

Ivan almost choked on his candyfloss when he saw Laura Idlewild flying past in her blue bra. The clowns had just run off, squirting each other with water, the lights grew dim and some trumpet music had started to play. She appeared in a single spotlight as suddenly as if she had jumped straight through the roof of the tent. The throbbing of the generators grew louder with the rising trumpet and she swung out over their heads, arching her back. She was silver in the spotlight, surprisingly muscular: practically naked right in front of his eyes. Back and forth across the big top she swung, with powerful pulses of her body sending the trapeze swooping ever higher, her spangles twinkling. Ivan gasped, nudged Angus.

'Look, it's Laura,' he said. His head was being drawn back and forth like a cat watching a bird.

'Don't be so stupid,' Angus said, elbowing him back but not breaking his gaze.

Laura flipped upside down like a rubber band and hung by her feet, cascade of long blonde hair flying.

'It is,' Ivan insisted, prodding him a bit harder, but Angus told him to shut up and jabbed him, a proper shove so it actually hurt, and she went flying past, dancing her arms through the air like she was conducting a choir of trumpet-blowing angels.

He was on the edge of his seat. It *was* Laura. And her bum was bare! She stayed high above them for a while, waving her arms, and then swooped from her perch and out into thin air, so that everyone watching held their breath until she'd caught a second swing that a man in the wings had sent out. She grabbed it with both hands and performed another elastic flip that saw her fly, holding on to the trapeze while doing the splits, a heel and a pointed toe either side of her head, and the audience gasped at her good timing, though none as loudly as Ivan.

She jigged from foot to foot, pointing her toes and sticking out first one buttock and then the other, a bit like the pee pee dance, he thought. Bolts of white cloth descended from the ceiling and she wound them around herself, coiling into the centre of a cocoon, this way and that, with various somersaults and stuff, and then descended, twirling and jerking; unrolling from the white silk, falling at some speed head first to the floor, stopping just short of it. Ivan stood up from his seat, heart thumping, and Laura freed herself with a slow, muscular back flip, first one nutcracker leg followed by the other, to face the audience and take her bow, blue bra, teeth, eyes and spangly bits sparkling.

Angus was spluttering, laughing and pointing instead of

clapping: 'He thinks that's Laura,' he said to their mum, who leaned over to ruffle Ivan's hair, and then annoyingly tucked it behind his ears. 'He does so love Laura,' said his dad, who was sitting next to him, and he began to laugh too, which started Ivan's eyes stinging.

There was a clown who kept falling over his own feet, and white horses who galloped by, ostrich plumes streaming, a juggler who dropped one of his fire clubs and swore under his breath. All Ivan could think about was Laura up on that trapeze. Why would she keep it secret? When he was in the circus he'd tell everyone. Ivan intended to be the Strong Man. Angus always thought he couldn't pick him up but he proved him wrong when he carried him right across the sitting room. He could probably lift up Laura if she'd let him. Angus was wrong about lots of things, but he acted all the time like he knew everything. Ivan nudged him in the ribs just because he felt like it.

'Ouch, what?'

'Stop, Ivan,' said their mother, holding up a hand. 'Let's have a good time without squabbling.'

The finale was a tiny child dressed in a Spanish costume of red and black lace and six little palomino ponies with dainty feet who bowed down before her like fat blond courtiers, before the whole troupe marched by, waving, in a razzle of feathers and sequins and some rousing music that people clapped along to and Ivan was standing again, craning his neck. Her blonde hair was unmistakable, down past her shoulders, flowing out behind her with a long blue sparkly cape to match her blue bra. She looked right across at him as he waved.

★

He was the king of the road. No stabilisers now he was a big boy, and Laura seemed to have forgotten that he was supposed to wear a helmet so he could feel the breeze in his hair. Laura could barely keep up, he could pedal so fast; she had to jog, which made her cheeks pink and the lace on one of her trainers had come undone. She called out for him to stop and he wobbled, but only a little bit. He braked beside a once-white van. Someone had written in finger on the grime: *If my wife was this dirty I'd stay at home*. He could read! He could read anything he wanted.

'Slow down a bit, Ivan.' She was puffing as she bent down at the kerb to do up her trainer. 'I can't keep running.' Some golden locks of hair had escaped from under her beanie hat and fell across her pink cheeks. Laura stood from tying her lace and pushed the escaped strands back beneath the blue beanie. 'What does that mean?' He pointed to the writing on the grubby van. She snorted, 'I'm only the babysitter, it's not part of the job . . .' but she didn't explain. 'Mr Speedy,' she called him.

He was fast as a rocket on his yellow bike. He could disappear in a cloud of dust. Hey presto. Everything coming at him like a set of new magic tricks. He could read, he could ride a bike, he could swim without armbands, soon he'd be able to fly. Nothing would ever surprise him again.

Angus got a new bike as soon as Ivan learned to ride. He never stopped going on about it. It had gears. Ivan was sick about the gears. But this old bike was yellow, his favourite colour, and it had a very loud bell.

'Come on, Buster,' she said, setting off again at a loping trot, so her small pink rucksack bounced up and down.

'Race you,' she called over her shoulder, speeding up as they headed into the village, uphill, along the Long Road.

She slowed to a walk and he kept pedalling to overtake her. She was puffing again. 'I don't think I can run all the way,' she said. 'Don't let me have a doughnut.' He wondered if Angus was having fun at his stupid friend Dominic's Laser Quest party.

She made him get off to walk when they turned into the pedestrian street. It was really annoying having to push the bike and the pedal kept catching him on the back of his leg.

Angus got to go in Uncle Tim's car. Lucky. 'Ruffians,' he called them. 'Anything so your poor parents can grab a weekend away,' he said when he came, a hand grabbing each of them by the scruff of the neck, pretending to bang their heads together so Laura laughed.

Ivan didn't quite trust Uncle Tim not to bang their heads. Tim often tickled Ivan a little more than he liked. On the plus side he did contribute regularly and generously to the extensive arsenal upstairs. He gave them guns that screeched and pinged and flashed lights and some that sounded like an entire amusement arcade all on their own. Their mum always gave him the look. 'Arms dealer,' she said. Not friendly.

He wasn't grey, which was odd because he and their dad were twins. Their dad never joined in with the bows and arrows and catapults, or the various water weapons and guns that shot foam discs, bits of potato, rubber bands, bendy darts, soft yellow pellets, stinging red ones, but Uncle Tim let them stalk him around the house. Sometimes they got a good long shot at him but more often than not he was too quick and charged them to the ground, wrestling the guns from their hands and shooting them back. Uncle Tim said his hair was still brown because he didn't have children or a wife to shout at him. 'It's because you don't have a conscience,' their mum said. Uncle Tim always roared over the humpback bridge out of the village, thrilling them: 'Hold on to your willies, boys!'

Ivan looked at Laura chewing the skin from the edge of her thumb. 'Have you been in the circus this week?'

She didn't even smile or break her stride or look at him. She just sighed: 'What do you think?'

'Is your trapeze still broken in bits?'

'Oh, Ivan.'

'Have the dancing budgies hatched their eggs?'

She grinned at him then and laughed, her earrings danced. 'Ivan, you don't forget a single detail,' she said. He looked at her again, sideways from under his fringe, trying to see what was funny. She was still smirking; he could see her big gappy teeth. Doubt started to point a hot finger at his chest. 'Oh, Ivan!' she said again. As soon as they got home he planned to challenge her to a contest out on the monkey bars, then he'd know for sure.

She'd been a bit strange all afternoon, laughing all the time. Tim had brought Cadburys' Flakes when he came for Angus, even one for her, but then he kept putting her off when she was about to take a bite by singing the advert under his breath: '*Only the crumbliest, flakiest chocolate . . .*' and for some reason that was so funny that she couldn't bite it for laughing and looking at him and bits of it flew down her front.

Laura liked sweets almost as much as Ivan did. Once, when she was reading him a story, she had broken off bits of his Easter egg and eaten them, which was basically stealing. She liked milk chocolate, and Dime bars best, but for him and Angus she brought forbidden, brightly coloured sweets like the giant swirly E numbers on sticks, in return for them leaving her alone to get on with her Facebook.

'Don't tell your mum and dad,' she said when she tore off the wrappers. He imagined she got them from the sweet stall at the circus. He wondered if she had to pay or if circus performers were allowed to have as many free sweets as they liked. Laura even smelled of sweets, her skin deliciously of warm candyfloss, which did nothing to quell his desire to burrow himself into the softest bits of her at every opportunity.

They turned left by Budgens and she said, 'Just need to get some cig . . .' She was too well brought-up to say the word in front of him. He'd never caught her smoking; perhaps she put them out in her pocket. The circus magician had probably taught her how. Probably everyone in the circus smoked. The juggler and the clowns and the ringmaster. But not the señorita child with the blond ponies who Ivan now knew to be a forty-six-year-old midget called Bridget and not a child at all. She was Laura's best friend in the circus.

'Have they mended your trapeze yet?'

The newsagent was grumpy about the bike, but he couldn't very well leave it outside. He looked up at her secreting the packet of cigarettes in her rucksack. Her sparkly fish earring had silver scales that shimmered as she shook her head, like it might be about to curl up its tiny tail and tell your fortune.

'Oh, Ivan, not this again.' She was still laughing and ignoring his question.

He shrugged. Angus was probably having much more fun than him. There would be hot dogs with squeezy red and yellow sauce bottles which they would squirt at each other.

'Why do we have to go to the café?' he grumbled. He kicked a stone and just missed her leg. This was the first time he'd ever got her all to himself. Angus always like a great big orange feather duster in his face, annoying him and making him look stupid. 'Oooh, Laura, Ivan loves you! Ivan thinks you're hot!' so that he wished someone would come and adopt him. 'Well?'

'Why don't we talk about something other than the circus,' she said.

'But I want to know because when your trapeze is mended you won't have time to babysit and I won't see you any more.' Tears had sprung to his eyes.

'Well,' she said, giving in. 'I will have to practise rather a lot . . .'

The café was steamy with customers; they grabbed the table in the window as soon as it became free. She went to the counter to get them cakes and he thought of her on her trapeze all the time like him on the monkey bars, no time to spare. Another thing he can do that he didn't used to be able to: he can hang upside down by his knees from the bars. And sit up and grab the bar with his hands, and do a roly-poly over it. Until last weekend, all impossible. Angus went round and round over the monkey bars all the time and Ivan had to pretend he didn't even want to hang upside down. Now he couldn't wait to show Laura his impression of a bat.

Laura brought cake and hot chocolate. Jennifer, that was the midget's second name. Bridget Jennifer, she was called. He wondered if her little blond ponies had been returned to her yet.

Laura took a bite of cake, leaving chocolate crumbs on her chin. She said that Bridget Jennifer's ponies had been taken hostage by a rival circus and dyed bright pink.

She smiled and nicked some of the cake he hadn't been quick enough to eat. She was giving in, he could tell. He loved to see her dimples, loved to poke his fingers into them. 'Bridget Jennifer is so distraught she is unable to play her maracas,' she said, glancing out of the window, then pointing and whispering: 'Look, Ivan, here comes someone.'

They had fun at the café. With Ivan as look-out, Laura had superglued a one-pound coin to the pavement outside. Laura's eyes looked like the blue might overflow, she laughed so much. Ivan's lemonade shot out of his nose when two bigger boys from his school, in football shirts, tried to kick the coin free, but later he felt a little sad when an old lady came along, checked that there was no one watching behind her, and hitched up her skirts in order to kneel on the pavement.

He asked Laura again about the state of her trapeze.

'The chains are still in pieces; Health and Safety won't hear of me going back, so they'll have to make do with the tightrope walker for a while longer.' She yawned, and then he wasn't sure if she was laughing at him or at the old lady who was rearranging her skirts as she went on her way.

'Is that the tightrope walker called Twinkle Periwinkle with the little pink dogs?'

'Oh, Ivan,' she said, giggling again as she picked cake crumbs from her plate with the end of her finger. 'You are persistent. Yes, it's Twinkle on the tightrope and you'll never guess what . . .?'

'What?' Oh, he loved Laura.

'Her little pink dog has just had little pink puppies!' Laura was the best.

She was better than any of the babysitters that came later. There was Claudine, for a while, who ignored them, headphones clamped to her ears, lost in the teeming jungle of her iPhone, and now they had Lola who was damp and pale and about as interesting as washing. Lola looked like her stringy arms would snap if she ever hung from monkey bars.

He'd never got Laura out there. It'd started to rain on the way back from the café. 'Too wet, we'll slip,' she said, shaking her bright hair free of the beanie. He never got another chance to test her.

His mum said: 'Laura's never available. I think I might as well stop asking. There's always some excuse: piano practice, exams . . .'

He stared at a painting he and Laura had done, a life-size cut-out of himself, still Blu-Tacked, hanging like an old map on the back of the kitchen door. It gave him a feeling like homesickness whenever he stopped to look at it.

Ivan knows why Laura doesn't come any more.

'Perhaps she won the lottery and doesn't need the money,' their dad said.

She'd unrolled a sheet of old wallpaper from the cupboard under the stairs and got Ivan to lie down on it. He had to hold out his arms and legs and keep still while she drew around him with a crayon. It tickled where it touched him, and he felt something quite powerfully that he didn't yet have a name for. Like butterflies. They painted blue for his jeans, green for his sweatshirt. She did the eyes and he did the mouth.

'Or did the boys do something terrible to her? Ivan? Angus?'

He still got the butterflies a bit to think about the crayon touching the inside edges of his legs. Did his mum really think he and Angus would do something so bad that Laura Idlewild wouldn't want to come back?

They'd fought, it was true, but she was used to that. Things had been thrown within minutes of Angus's return from Laser Quest, him swaggering in with a piece of creamy cake in a box, a floating yellow balloon with a design of a Laser Quest gun on it, a man-sized Laser Quest T-shirt with POWER written in big letters. The T-shirt was as big as battledress and Angus wore it over his own clothes so he looked bulky. Ivan wanted to tell him about the coin they'd superglued to the pavement. Angus was too busy showing off. Uncle Tim all the time quizzing Laura about everything: what she likes to eat, what she drinks. 'Vodka cranberry' made him cackle. 'Not a lightweight then?' About friends, Facebook. 'You kids, there's no mystery. You know everything there is to know about each other already. What's the point of going on a date?' Angus goofing around with a stuffed gonky toy with toilet-brush hair as orange as his own. The toy also wearing a Laser Quest T-shirt. It was intolerable: Angus's going-home presents were considerably more lavish than the proper present he'd taken for the birthday boy.

Tim said: 'Strewth, Laura. Show a man some mercy. At least open a bottle of wine, I know Simon's got something drinkable stashed somewhere. I've never seen so many savages. Angus has turned into a maniac.'

But *he* was the maniac. He came creeping up behind her when she was staring into the fridge, half hanging off the door, in the way she did when she was snackish.

'Hey Laura . . . What do you expect to find in there?' She jumped because she didn't know he was in the room. 'Dreamboy isn't about to come roaring through the butter dish on his Harley, you know!'

Ivan had been standing at the fruit bowl. He saw how Uncle Tim made her blush. He was so rude. She was uncomfortable, caught out like a shoplifter, but his mum had said she could help herself to anything she fancied. He shouted, 'Catch!' at Uncle Tim, and lobbed an orange at his head, just missing him.

The orange rolled away across the floor and Uncle Tim shoved the cat, Cato, off the table, something that would never have happened if his mother had been home. 'Go on, you filthy thing,' Tim said, sending him off, astonished, tail flicking.

Laura let them play Twister when they were in their pyjamas. This was after their fight with the creamy cake and once Uncle Tim had made Ivan clear up the mess because he was the one who'd thrown it. 'I'm the future King, I'm the heir, you're just the spare!' Things had only got worse since Angus started learning history at school. Laura helped him clean up the splatted cake. She didn't always take Angus's side like everyone else.

Laura was in charge of spinning the dial. 'Ivan, right arm

on blue; Angus, left leg on yellow', and they tangled around each other until somehow Angus's bum was right in Ivan's face and he farted and Ivan couldn't move because he was being squashed by Uncle Tim who had joined in. He could barely breathe for the stink and Angus wouldn't stop laughing.

Laura took him upstairs to cool down. She told him about the time that she put a marshmallow in her brother's bum — 'Right between the cheeks' — to pay him back for being mean to her. 'When Ed woke up in the morning he didn't know what was going on! It was a pink marshmallow, I'd saved it specially.' Ivan couldn't stop himself laughing when she told him. 'All melted so he thought he had a disease!'

Ivan had managed to make her come to his bedside twice more after that. Once with hot chocolate and then later, when he insisted that he couldn't sleep, she had pulled his head on to her chest and stroked his hair and told him more about the pink puppies and Bridget Jennifer and about the palomino ponies with their muzzles as soft as velvet.

Lola arrived looking like a parsnip, all pale and scraggy. Their mum and dad were grabbing last-minute things: tickets, car keys, his mum was dithering about whether to take her camera. Angus was pretending to do his homework on the computer but Ivan knew he'd be straight on to a game the minute they left and stringy Lola would do nothing about it. Ivan stared longingly at the painted cut-out that Laura had made, at his yellow hair all whipped up like icing on a cake, his blue legs. You could see the black line of her crayon where she drew round him. The painting looked quite scruffy now. People kept going in and out and it had lost a hand, but still it made him get goosebumps.

He'd been woken from a dream that night: in the ring, he could smell the sawdust. Laura and him riding the fat blond ponies, there'd been cheering from the wings. There was the sound of a bottle being knocked over and he could hear peals of laughter downstairs. Cato came screeching to a halt in his bedroom, scuttering the rug.

He could see Angus lying in his bed by the window, mouth a little open, soft adenoidal snores, safely in the land of nod. Ivan followed Cato on tiptoes down the stairs.

They were playing Twister. He could see them quite clearly from the bottom of the stairs. They were in darkness but for the fire which had been lit with a roaring flame. He could smell the wood and he could smell that they'd been smoking. Their legs were entwined on the mat. Tim reached over her to spin the arrow and she laughed as though she'd been tickled. 'Left arm on red.' They were both snorting with laughter but Ivan couldn't work out what was so funny. Right leg on yellow. Left leg on green. She was on her hands and knees beneath him. Right leg on blue. She was breathtaking: hands and feet barely losing contact with the correctly coloured discs, she was flipping herself over and arching into a perfect crab, head thrown back and her hair pouring like honey over the Twister mat. Tim tried to keep his balance with his left leg over Laura's right, grabbed at her and then fell into a heap. She collapsed on top of him, laughing, and Ivan saw her shirt fall open and saw that she was wearing her blue bra.

The Rose
Before the Vine

The man at the next table asked for tap water as though it was a special virtue and in a voice far louder than the one he'd used ordering wine. Self-satisfied twit, Rose thought, as under the table she eased her swollen feet from her shoes.

She'd already asked the waiter for San Pellegrino and her feet ached along with the rest of her, enough to make her despise everyone there. The couple in the window had brought their baby along, its plastic rattle too. A *vegetarian* restaurant. How typical of Anna to have picked it. Rose couldn't remember wanting to sink her teeth into a steak quite so much before in her life.

She'd eaten her way through a whole bowlful of flaccid olives, she'd even started to pick at the salt crystals in their little bowl; soon there would be only pepper left to sustain her.

Rose called for some bread but lacked confidence in the

waiter. Incy Wincy Spider incessantly, and percussively, climbed the waterspout. She checked her watch. Officially late. Anna, you always had to shout at her. Rose stemmed a wave of sudden panic that maybe she wouldn't turn up at all. Anna, the one to hide just one of her shoes in the attic, or go missing herself, just at the point that everyone was trying not to miss the bus.

Infuriating of the girl to have suggested somewhere so unpeaceful. Rose longed to be back in Italy, free of this dismal place and the burden she was in it to deliver. It was more than a prophecy, weightier than a hunch; it came with statistics that hung like a bag of nails in her heart and still no sign of Anna, annoying girl that she'd always been.

How ugly the people were. Tap water man had the sort of looks that made her think that his own birth might not have been a pleasant one: eyes close together in a head shaped like a hillock, flock of dark hair taking flight; and his wife neat as a tulip, probably put her pale clothes on fresh from the packet each morning.

The special of the day was haloumi cheese pretending to be chip-shop fish. Chunky chips. Mushy peas. Her stomach made an embarrassingly enthusiastic gurgle. She'd order that, should Anna ever deign to appear. Always missing. Too often missing from Rose's memories.

'Mama? What's wrong?' She hadn't noticed her come in and the breath of her made her jump. She'd been busy eavesdropping on tap water couple, who were on the brink of an argument. Anna was a sprite on her feet, scruffy Balinese slippers, too thin; a bit of a mess as usual, all angles like Jimmy, hair roughly scrunched into a band. Rose didn't mean to cry, hurriedly blotted a couple of tears with the end of her sleeve.

'You have given me the fright of my life!' Anna fired at her before they'd caught their breath. 'Why so urgent?'

'I'll tell you,' she said.

They pecked each other's cheeks, left and right, a courtly dance. They almost hugged: they both thought about it then let their arms fall.

'Well?'

As they pulled the chairs back their eyes met for the first time in over a year: Anna's big and grey, sad always, even when she smiled. Rose's sadder still because she couldn't look at Anna without seeing how her future lay, the darkness of the pit that she would fall into.

'What's the big mystery?' Anna's elbows sharp as she rolled up the sleeves of an oddly shapeless garment, rubbing her long forearms. 'What are you doing turning up here like this?'

Rose pulled her knitted collar closer around her neck; the sight of Anna almost made her shiver. Anna so wraith-like: as a child she could disappear into thin air. One hot day, all playing hide and seek in the vineyard, they'd lost her for an entire afternoon, shouted themselves hoarse. It was almost dark when she reappeared and she never told them where she'd been.

'Is everyone all right? Is Massimo OK?'

Rose nodded. 'Of course Massimo's all right,' she said, blowing her nose on the napkin and wondering if a secret part of Anna hoped that he wouldn't be. 'He still gets out for a walk every day.'

Massimo, the marauding Roman who'd leapt into

Jimmy's shoes too soon after his death, and dragged them all off across the sea to his lair. It was easy to imagine that they might see him like that. Especially this suspicious daughter winding the loop of her shoulder bag around the back of her chair, in case it should be stolen. Little Anna who came running back and saw how Massimo kissed her when he walked her from Jimmy's grave.

Anna was apologising for being late, something to do with her work. The row on the next table was reaching its crescendo: 'Life would be a lot easier if you didn't keep having to go abroad all the bloody time,' Mr Tap Water's wife said in a whiney voice, like a child.

'Stop staring!' Anna hissed.

Abroad all the bloody time was precisely where Rose wanted to be; she was chilled to the marrow as only the English seaside could make her. She longed to be in the warm folds of her house in Castagnola, the soft earth with its smell of the forest, the river just starting to flow, the leaves falling, Massimo's pipe smoke, an elegant decay all around. All she'd ever wished was that her girls should marry Italians.

'Food first, we need to order.' Rose held up a finger, silencing Anna's questions. 'Talk after that.'

The least she could do was to try to feed the poor thing up. Anna made her think of a bedraggled pigeon.

Anna bent her head to study the menu and Rose thought at first that she was mistaken by the silver glintings in the looped-up nest of hair, just one or two here and there. She didn't feel ready to be the mother of a daughter whose hair was going grey.

Anna recommended a salad, typically for one so thin.

'I wish they wouldn't employ people like him,' Rose said as the waiter approached. 'It could put people off their dinner.'

Anna stared at her. 'Don't you care if he hears you?' Her daughter's disapproval, sharp as a slap. Rose could feel her cheeks going red already and her bones almost ached to be in front of the fire in Castagnola.

There was that English saying, wasn't there? A girl's your daughter for the rest of her life. A boy's your son until he finds a wife. Rose snorted at the injustice. Anna was stuck, had been since she was a little slip of eighteen, clinging like a barnacle to the underside of this grim seaside town. Rose hated its Victorian pretensions: the fallacy of ornamental piping on facades hiding stacked-up bedsits and rising damp.

These dreary and unfortunate Isles held nothing but bad memories. The dusty smell of the rain and lumpy stew with strings of gristle, the sting of a slipper, slam of a door, a dank room with a carved crucifix on the wall. Her first husband, Jimmy, and three little tots to bear witness to his slow yellowing, until sinew was all that separated skin and bones. He looked like he was being crucified, silently screaming, as the children hung on her arms, her thighs, always someone on her lap, almost bruising her they clung so hard, and his refusal to give in right up to the end, the way his ghost's hand still pushed away the morphine.

England: like a bad dream. The repulsive waiter brought their food, long shoes slapping across the floor, pale and slightly sweaty as though he'd been poaching too long in his own juices.

Anna was wearing dark leggings with a shapeless flappy

wool thing and a thin grey T-shirt through which her breasts poked like little mushrooms. At least there wouldn't be much to miss, Rose thought grimly.

'What is the dreadful thing you've discovered?' Anna pulled at the sleeves of the thin woolly, reminding Rose how hard she'd always been on her clothes as a child. 'You've found out who your parents were, is that it?'

Rose nodded, pulled at her own more substantial cardigan.

'And it's not good news.'

Anna said she knew that much. She'd already spoken to her sister. 'I know when Tilda's trying not to cry, I could hear how she kept having to swallow.'

Fresh tears came stinging to Rose's eyes and she had to dab them again, just to have a thought of Tilda. How carefree she'd been, only last night, dancing around with that putto of hers before Rose had come crashing in and ruined everything with her news. Tilda, so warm and oily from her bath. The naked baby boy on her hip, a regular cherub, the pair of them like Titian's *Madonna and Child*. The smooth glow of her skin, all gleaming curves; God preserve. Tilda calling to her, their arms entwined, cherub and all. The sweet baby smell of her skin. 'Mama' being whispered in her ear.

Anna was pushing some sprouted things around her plate; there were small ladders at the seams of her flappy jumper, she always had looked like she was falling to bits. Tilda you could put in white and it'd stay white all day, she didn't come home in rags like Anna.

'You are too thin,' Rose said, exasperating her, making her reach up and twist her hair more tightly into its band.

Tilda's child was a regular cherub. He ran towards Rose, gloriously naked from his bath, escaping the towel that had been wrapped around him. '*Ciccio!*'

Tilda laughed, that chuckle of hers, lovely round naked shoulders, copper hair falling in waves about them, some still pinned up, generous body draped in a towel. 'A real little fatty,' she said.

The child was ablaze with Titian curls, slippery-naked, wriggling himself into her arms like a puppy. '*Ti sei fatto male quando sei caduto giù dal cielo?*'

'Did you hurt yourself when you fell from heaven?' Tilda translated for her Danny boy, ruffling his hair.

'*Ciccio*, fatty, *bello* . . .' Rose was unable to stop herself from pinching bits of him like dough and chuckling too, feeling her daughter's arms enfold her, cherub and all, and then standing for a moment, a trio, and imagining that all around them there had been a heavenly glow.

'So, what did you find out?' Anna prompted. 'Who were they? What's the big mystery?' Rose took a gulp of water, wondered if Anna looked like any of her ancestors; she certainly hadn't inherited much from Rose. For all she knew Rose's own mother and grandmother were boyish too. That was one of the problems with being an orphan: never being able to look through the telescope from the other end.

She thought again of Tilda through the bathroom door, not like Anna at all. Rose had seen as she unwound her towel, Venus, young and plump, emerging, pale-skinned and lovely as a moon.

'Turns out my mother was not a whore from the back-streets of Dublin, after all!' she said.

'Why would you think she was?' Anna's eyes widened.

'She was a hard-working farm girl from County Kerry who married a soldier. It's a pity no one found any pictures. Bernadette and Donal O'Docherty.'

'They have names!' Anna reached across the table and shook Rose's shoulder. 'How does that feel?' Rose remembered how hard it was to maintain eye contact with this daughter.

'It's a mercy the Sisters of Mercy let us see the files after all the asking,' she said. Anna's eyes made her think of a starving child they were so large in her face.

'But, there's a terrible thing . . .'

'So?'

Rose waved a hand irritably around the restaurant, indignant as a teacher in a noisy classroom: 'I can't tell you here with all these people.'

Mother, grandmother, both aunts; probably more, the whole family riddled with it. Jimmy's lot, too: mother and sister.

'Did someone murder someone? Is that it? Should I start suffering from ancestor shame right away?' Anna started to giggle.

Rose shook her head, she couldn't do this right now. The DNA time bomb would have to wait. 'Later,' she said. 'I want to know how you are. We haven't spoken for so long.'

'Hurry up and eat then come back to the flat,' Anna said. 'Tell me whatever the big bad secret is when we get there.' She seemed to bounce a little in her seat. 'And I can show you what I've been working on.' Anyone would think she suffered from arrested development. Still dresses like a teenager. Such rags! And fingers all inky blue for some reason. Mortuary blue; Rose couldn't suppress an internal shudder.

'Natural indigo,' Anna said, noticing Rose's gaze and holding her hands above the table and wiggling them as though she were playing an invisible keyboard. 'Stains everything.'

Ah, yes. It never failed to astonish Rose that Anna had become the artist of the family; that Anna's hand-dyed rag rugs hung on the walls of galleries in London and Amsterdam. It seemed the world couldn't get enough of them. The one Anna had made for Rose some years before was pleasant enough and was currently employed as a bath mat, and a very nice bath mat it was too.

The baby in the window had possession of the rattle; tap water man was defending his need to travel. Why would anyone want to live with you twelve months of the year anyway? sneered his wife; plates were being crashed about. There was a chicken-kiev-style outpouring of liquid grease when Rose cut into the battered haloumi.

'So, your parents? Are you going to tell me anything?' Anna pushed her long fringe behind her ears. Her daughter's eyes were a storm colour that shifted uneasily between blue and grey; even early on Rose had felt judged; even when she was breastfeeding Anna, the cold, unblinking marble of her baby eye had the power to spook her.

Rose's other children all had brown eyes; it had taken some getting used to. Jimmy had promised to haunt her, and he did.

She told Anna some of what she knew about Bernadette O'Docherty. 'My mama,' she said, and immediately felt foolish for saying it.

Rose had been found clinging to Bernadette's dying body. 'There was no one else to take me, her own mother already in the grave and my father killed in the war before I was even born.'

Bernadette died alone, in agony probably. 'The Sisters of Mercy took me when she became too weak to lift me.' Rose tried to stem a rising tide of anger, or grief, she wasn't sure which. There, she wanted to say to Anna, give that to your shrink from me: tell him to stick all that in his pipe and smoke it, the next time he decides to conjure up Jung or Freud or whoever while you moan about your child-hood and he theorises about me.

It was only a light drizzle when they got outside, just a short walk, Anna said. She took Rose's arm, waved at the sodium lights on their tall posts with their halos shimmer-ing on the black wet streets all the way up the hill, sighed: 'It is beautiful here, don't you think?'

Rose shivered, hoped it wouldn't be far, her feet couldn't take it. The porches of the houses had fluted pillars; there were curlicues and garlands. The plasterwork reminded Rose of her first wedding cake, the one she'd cut with Jimmy, a struggle to get the knife through the cold white icing, three tiers. A piece brought out like a prize with tea and silver spoons at the christenings of Leo, Tilda and then finally, though Jimmy's moods by that time made her feel less than celebratory, Anna.

Rose couldn't manage to walk these streets and talk at the same time. 'Better with a brandy,' she said.

Rose's Italian wedding cake had been a different affair: messy, glistening; a pyramid of creamy profiteroles, piled up in a generous heap, caramel-coloured as the sun-baked houses in Castagnola; sticky and sweet as any metaphor for love. She couldn't wait to be back. Massimo's was the only shoulder that she allowed herself to cry on.

She thought of him collecting pine cones for the hearth, out there in the forest, poking around with the end of his stick, hoping to find a truffle, as likely as a four-leaf clover, but he was the lucky sort, grinning slightly foolishly, wearing his thick knitted scarf the colour of ripe tomatoes. Rose felt a little warmer just thinking of him as Anna led her left into Evrika Street.

'Is it much further?' Rose asked, puffing slightly, regretting her inability to lose a couple of stone.

'Do you not remember that this is my road?' Anna stalled, a little huffy.

'Evrika Street, of course!' Rose's last visit had not been a success. It had only been for one afternoon; on the way back from Tilda's then, too, and a small crumb of conversation to go with the cup of tea that Anna plonked down in front of her would not have gone amiss, instead of the reproachful ragtime she bashed out on the piano.

The piano practically shook the wall of Anna's miserable sitting room. Rose remembered sitting with the tea cooling in the cup, saucer on her knees, cushions crackling with resentment, the rain beetling down the windows while Anna played relentlessly on. She was certainly no Oscar Peterson, her daughter.

When she finally stopped – it had taken her several attempts to play the piece right through – Rose had apparently failed to tell her well done.

'Why didn't you let me have piano lessons when I was little?' Rose couldn't for the life of her remember turning her down. Leo, yes, he'd played, so had Tilda; Anna, not really. Rose had held back a childish urge to mutter 'Diddums' as Anna went on about it. As far as Rose was concerned she held all the trump cards herself: being an orphan, *clinging* to poor Bernadette's wasted body, that's what they said; passed to and fro, the bad luck of ending up with an adoptive mother so self-righteously cruel. Then, oh Lord above, Jimmy. The full hand, the whole miserable deck. *Piano lessons*. What was Anna's problem?

'I'm seeing a shrink.' Anna had said it as though that was perfectly all right and not a slight on her in the least. 'Every Thursday.' A shrink! Rose had felt it like a punch to the belly.

'It's not an insult! It's not like the RSPCA being called in about your dog, really it isn't!' Anna had tried to make a joke of it, to call her back. But Rose was already stalking off to an earlier train.

Evrika Street. Thank goodness, almost there. Rose was glad of her umbrella, a silky lime-green one, rather elegant, that Massimo had bought for her in Rome. Anna's hair hung in rats' tails because she had refused to come under it, said she didn't care if she got wet.

'I suppose you're in touch with your brothers? You'll know all their news. Leo's not been well.' Rain started to bounce from her umbrella. Anna shook water from her fringe as they stopped at her gate.

'Carla emails me about him.'

Rose didn't like to be reminded of Carla, Leo's wife, so possessive that Rose had to telephone her first to book it into her diary whenever she wanted to visit Leo in the hospital.

'And Cassio, do you hear from him?'

'Yes,' said Anna over her shoulder as she rummaged in her bag for keys, 'he calls me all the time.'

Again, a stab like jealousy. She'd been hoping most of all for siblings of her own when she'd started poking around in Ireland.

'By the way,' said Anna as she found her keys, 'there's something I didn't tell you in the restaurant.' She took a momentously deep breath, put the key in the lock: 'I've got a boyfriend.' Who, in their right mind, would put up with Anna? The question fell unbidden into her head and Rose was immediately ashamed of herself. Anna threw open the door.

'He's a bit nervous about meeting you,' she whispered over her shoulder and just for a moment Rose thought she was imagining the piano. But this wasn't playing like Anna's had been, it didn't stall and start and bash; it was without anger, and stopped with a cheerful trill as the front door clattered shut.

'Richard could have been a concert pianist,' Anna said, her eyes crinkling as he came into the hall.

A gangling man, as long in the limb as Anna: he was bending his fingers back at the knuckles, a couple of them cracked and then he held out his hand to her, blushing to the colour of a ripe pomegranate.

'Mama, this is Richard.' He was slightly stooped as though apologising for his height.

'It's good to meet you,' he said, a voice that was unusually quiet. For a moment as she looked up at him she saw a flare of light from the bulb in the hall behind his head, like a heavenly aura, and was reminded of the time she'd

seen a real halo: it had been shimmering around a neighbour, someone she'd been told to call Auntie Jean. Auntie
Jean had forced open the door to the windowless room
with the crucifix, found Rose there. She'd been more than
a day and a night by that time without food or water, not
even a bucket to pee in. Auntie Jean had come to get Rose
out, she held her against her comfortable apron, patted her
head, tried to keep her.

Richard took Rose's coat. He shook it a little to dry it,
and then Anna's. He had a rather elegant neck, long and
tender like a stem and with a prominent Adam's apple; he
might have swallowed the parson's nose. Or bitten off more
than he could chew, Rose thought, then felt ashamed all
over again.

'You should have called and I would've collected you in
the car.' Richard looked at Anna, not quite admonishing.
Rose noticed a smile pass between them as he hung their
coats on a hook.

Richard played so that her heart ached. 'Don't stop,' she
said when he reached a pause in the music. His expressive
phrasing made Anna's shoddy upright sound fit for a queen.
Anna had put Rose to sit on the sofa while she went for
brandy and glasses, a towel for her hair.

'I like this one,' Rose said, smiling and nodding a little,
and Anna slotted in beside her among the cushions. They
lifted the brandy to their lips while Richard played Chopin.

Richard had lit all the candles ready for when they came
in, he'd created a lovely dancing light. Even the ones in the
piano's candlelabrum were blazing so Rose feared that he
might catch his dark curls alight as he played.

The embers of a small fire warmed the grate and one of

Anna's rugs hung from the rail above. It seemed to glow, as though a breeze ruffled its colours, its russets and reds, oranges and ochres and earths, and Rose wasn't sure if she was imagining it, but then Anna confirmed in a whisper: 'Can you see what the colours are? In that rug? It's Castagnola. Castagnola in autumn. I've been working on it all year.'

Rose put her arm up and Anna let her head fall to her shoulder while Richard's playing grew quieter and then reached back up towards a crescendo, phrases repeating themselves, melodies threading in and out of each other, calling, repeating. Anna scooped down into the cushions until her head lay in Rose's lap.

'I was thinking about the vineyard.' Anna's eyes were closed, her pale eyelids finely veined and mauve like rose petals.

'I was thinking how much I used to like it there. There was a little hollow two thirds of the way down, it happened to be where two of the vines met so was completely obscured from view. I used to go there with a book.' Anna slid her feet along the sofa while Rose stroked her hair.

'I remember the rose bushes in the vineyard, so many different sorts. One bush planted at the end of each line. Why were they planted there? I don't think I ever knew.'

Rose could see the blue veins at Anna's temples as she stroked her hair back. 'It's tradition,' she said. 'The rose before the vine. Some people say they were planted there because they were thorny and discouraged the plough horses from trampling the vines.'

'Once when I was little I went out with scissors and cut a whole bunch of different roses for you,' Anna said. 'They were all very thorny. There were some dark red ones with prickles all along the stems like brambles, and lots of different pinks and oranges; my hands got cut.' Anna was talking, her head still in her mother's lap, knees curled up and the lovely music slurring and pattering. 'Shsh,' said Rose, gesturing at Richard playing a quiet passage where the notes seemed to grow misty.

Rose thought she would cry; the tune was swooping around the room and Anna's rug with its burnished colours seemed to blaze.

She thought of Anna at little Cassio's bath time, funny the things that slip into one's head. Perhaps it was seeing Tilda bath with her cherub that reminded her. Anna demanding to get into the bath too. Cassio's little towel with the bunny ears, how cute he looked in it, such a *ciccio*, just as much a little fatty as Tilda's boy. And there was Anna, out of the bath and dripping, all skinny, putting it on over her head, how hideous it looked, her front teeth grown big and too much like a rabbit's for the bunny ears to look anything other than charmless, the whole thing too short to cover her pudenda, twiggy legs dancing around. Cassio crying and saying that she'd stolen his towel.

Anna sat up from her lap. 'Anyway, you were saying. The rose was planted in front of the vine to deter clumsy horses.'

'Maybe that was it,' said Rose quietly. 'Though other people believed that planting the rose there would act as an early warning system. The rose gets the same diseases as the grape but shows symptoms sooner.' Rose couldn't bear the poignancy of what she was saying. 'It isn't foolproof.' Sometimes you'd get a hardy one, like herself, like the canary down the mine that goes on singing. It was becoming hard to speak. The pin was almost out; she was like a terrorist, biding her time there in Anna's lovely room with the soft light and music.

'Hopefully the rose got ill in time for the vine to be treated and saved,' she said, her heart beating faster.

Anna leapt up from the sofa and draped herself lightly over Richard at the piano. The Nocturne started fading towards its inevitable conclusion. Richard played on, still managing to kiss Anna with the side of his mouth, sliding his eyes away from the keys to meet hers sideways on, but only for a moment.

Remote Control

'I wish we didn't have a television,' I said to Simon after a particular weekend of blaring cartoon, cheesy quiz show, soap and reality TV hell. All day Saturday while the rain hammered our forsaken garden Simon kept the TV loud enough to drown out the voices of our bored and bickering children. And yesterday, the sun tried its Sunday best to break through – at an annoying angle for the screen, so Simon drew the curtains.

'It's not what you watch that bothers me,' I said when he returned home this evening, delayed by yet another disorder with the trains, and headed straight for his temple, dinner held before him like an offering to the Great God Prime Time. 'It's the time you waste doing it.'

'What are you?' said Simon, shooing Cato the cat, who had been curled like a warm croissant in the comfy armchair that just happened to have the best view of the television. 'My mother?'

'Anyway, you watch it enough yourself,' he added, failing, as usual, to notice the little double flick that Cato gave with his tail before huffily stalking from the room.

How I wish I had a nice long tail like Cato's: flick, flick, I'd go. 'Here's your dinner, Simon. Kept nice and warm for you,' flick, flick. That neat little gesture, as anyone who actually takes the time to talk to a cat will tell you, is the feline equivalent of the V-sign. Eff off! Flick flick, up yours! Flick flick, what, shoo me away? Flick flick, stuff you!

Sighing in a way that only the sole breadwinner of a family can truly pull off, Simon lowered himself into what he liked to refer to as *his* chair, dinner plate balanced on his knees. The television had been left on standby, its red light bright with the promise of pleasures to come. By the way he stared straight ahead at the screen I could tell that food and conversation were not uppermost in his mind.

'You're home too late to even see the children,' I said. '*Again*,' I said.

Come to think of it I hadn't seen much of them since school myself and, judging by the spewing DVD boxes on the floor, it looked like Ivan and Angus had spent most of the afternoon in the company of the electronic faux-friend too. I knelt down to reunite the boxes with the discs.

'Perhaps you'd like me to make little home movies of them in future?' I said, feeling my spite rise. 'You could sit there and watch them in the advertising breaks. That way you'd be able to recognise them should you ever be the one to pick them up from school.'

'That would be helpful,' Simon said with a small laugh,

happily mixing his peas into the warmed-up mashed potato on his plate.

'Now, shush,' he said. 'It's time for *Stars and Their Drawers*.' Or something like that, how on earth am I supposed to keep track of the names of all Simon's programmes? The room, I noticed, had a flat-Cola sort of stench to it and I wondered if Cato had been peeing in the fireplace again, because of the rain. Soggy paws have never been Cato's thing.

'Why don't you just sit down for once?' Simon sighed again, his hand scrabbling fruitlessly among the papers and sweet wrappers strewn on the table by his chair. He knocked a half-eaten honey sandwich to the floor, and then, because he didn't find what he was looking for, Simon lost it, toddler-style. 'Urrrmphhh.' He flung himself back into his chair.

'Where's the cruddy troll?' he hollered, paraphrasing Angus's imitation from years ago of Simon in customary full TV-frenzy searching for the 'bloody control'. 'Cruddy troll' had seemed quite funny back then.

'Ivan! Angus!' he bellowed through the ceiling, as though we had a brace of recalcitrant teenagers lolling around up there, and not two sleepy little children.

Sometimes I think he comes home in the evening just to madden us.

I found comfort with Cato in the kitchen. My lovely warm kitchen with its big family table and Ivan and Angus's paintings on the walls and doors, Angus's half-drunk milk still on the table, the comforting purr of the fridge.

'What a hullabaloo,' said Cato, yawning pinkly. 'As for:

"cruddy troll", don't you think it's time to lay off the tragic malapropism or what?' I could tell he was rather pleased with his own verbal dexterity; 'malapropism' being a word that not many cats use.

'"Who's *hidden* the cruddy troll?" is the worst,' Cato added with a disdainful nod in the direction of the sitting room: 'So paranoid.'

Cato purred a little as I nubbled my biggest knuckle on the white hairs beneath his chin. Recently I've found that all my best conversations have been with Cato and this evening was no exception.

'Television will do for modern man what lead pipes did for the Romans, you mark my words,' he said as I scratched his little beard and felt my eyes well up. I would never dream of mentioning it to Cato but mortality being what it is there is an inherent sadness in our friendship (or anyone's with their cat, I suppose, or dog, too, if that's what you prefer). Wouldn't it be easier if it weren't seven of their years to one of ours? What will I do without him? Come to that, who will I talk to?

Cato snapped me out of my mawkish mood. He arched his back, and bared his fangs in a tigerish fashion as the sound of the *Stars and Their Drawers* countdown came whooping through the wall. Simon had evidently located his Holy Grail without Angus or Ivan's assistance.

'Even people staring at a blank wall have more brain activity than people watching television,' said Cato. 'I calculate that Simon's viewing habits probably mean his cerebellum barely quivers in its fug of alpha waves. Simon's brain's about as active as a blancmange,' he said.

It has always been soothing to find, in dear Cato, a true ally in the battlefield of the idiot box/electronic babysitter/mind–sucker/boob tube/goggle-box. Call it what you like.

'"Simon's plug-in drug" is what I call it,' said Cato as Ivan shuffled into the kitchen, wearing his duvet as a cloak. Ivan headed for the fridge, as though having been woken then shooed away by his father gave him special dispensation to eat after teeth.

'Ivan?'

Ivan adopted his Oliver face at the fridge door. He's such a tiny boy for his age it's often hard to refuse him food, though at that moment he was yawning.

'Dad woke me up,' he said. 'Can I have a chocolate mousse?'

I could hear Simon zapping through channels in the next room: studio audience laughter cut to a booming bejingled assurance that 'Nothing keeps a woman fresher', and back to the same, or maybe a whole different set of lemmings laughing.

'Dad said I could,' said Ivan, sniffing.

At that moment, quite unbidden, a vision exploded before my eyes: my steak mallet smashing the TV screen to smithereens. It was so bright, this flash, and so violent, that I almost shut the fridge door on Ivan's fingers. 'To bed,' I hissed and Ivan burst into tears.

'Fancy coming in this late, then waking the kids up,' said Cato, licking the pink tip of his nose as I was pouring apologetic milk of human kindness into the pan for Ivan's hot chocolate, following a penitent double dose of chocolate mousse.

'His father is perfectly capable of making hot chocolate, you know,' commented Cato, sitting on the table huffily pulling at his dew claws. 'Talk about remote control. I ask you . . .'

'Do you know what I do sometimes?' I said, deciding that I'd better divert Cato before he got too hissy. 'Sometimes when Simon's watching TV, I have a little game I play, you should come in and watch.' I told him how occasionally I amused myself by placing the remote control on the arm of my chair, just out of his reach, and then counting the seconds before Simon found an excuse to reclaim it.

'Uh-oh,' said Cato, in a rather drawly mid-Atlantic impersonation of Simon. 'Pass me the cruddy troll, would you, darling? I think the colour balance needs adjusting.'

Cato stretched out on the table and looked me full in the eyes. 'It's the children I worry about,' he said, returning to his normal voice. 'All that television must take a terrible toll on their IQs.'

A child can get away with anything if it learns to look an adult straight in the eyes. Angus and Ivan are both very good at direct eye contact. Not so Simon.

Simon hadn't managed to look at me once since our little fracas on Friday night when I informed him that I wanted to buy Cato something rather special for his birthday. The following may sound a little bonkers, but in my defence, Cato had been saying that he missed having someone of his own species to chat to. He kept mentioning some local Burmese kittens he'd heard about. Apparently they are *lilac* Burmese, a particularly attractive shade of pearly grey. (Cato says a Burmese would be best: there'd be a better chance of it turning out to be a Buddhist, like him.)

'I can't believe what I'm hearing,' Simon said as the children ran in, wet from the garden and rowdy as kittens themselves. 'Are you seriously telling me that you want to buy a kitten as a birthday present for the *cat*?'

'For Cato,' I said, realising as soon as the words left my lips that perhaps it did seem a tad unhinged. I felt a gust of cold air as the children failed to close the garden door. 'And let's not forget,' I added, grateful for the divine intervention of sudden inspiration, 'it's Ivan's birthday in under a month . . .'

Simon clutched his jaw in both hands. 'Ivan is having a new bike,' he said. Ivan, bless him, wrapped his arms around his father's knees. 'I want a kitten, I want a kitten,' he said. 'Yeah,' said Angus, hands on holsters and cowboy hat askew, 'and I'm having one too.'

After that Simon sulked for the rest of the weekend. He sat in that chair and brandished the remote control like a spray repellent.

I almost fell asleep when I took Ivan his hot chocolate. I lay upstairs in the children's dark bedroom, sharing a pillow with my little boy, his breath sweet as clover, with the comforting steadiness of Angus's breathing coming from the next bed. If it hadn't been for the shrilling of television adverts through the floorboards it might have been one of those sublime moments of a life. My two healthy children and me, all breathing together like the sea. Instead, Ivan started moaning that he'd never get to sleep with that racket, which woke Angus, who had a tantrum when I told him to go straight back to sleep because I didn't really feel like making further hot chocolate. 'It's not room service, you know', and below the television audience laughed and laughed.

Downstairs, suffering my usual capitulation at the sight of Angus's quivering baby blues, I began heating milk for more hot chocolate. As I reached for the whisk from the brown ceramic pot of utensils beside the cooker, Cato jumped on to the work surface and twined his tail around my arm.

'While you were upstairs,' he said in a stage whisper.

'Yes?'

'Well, you know how I hate to gossip,' he said. Cato can look quite kittenish when he's toying with something juicy. 'The thing is,' he said, rolling appealingly on to his side, 'I just overheard Simon on the phone, and he was ordering a Sky Box for the television.' The steak hammer swam into view. Cato appeared to be pointing to its wooden handle with the tip of his tail.

'Enough,' I cried. I grabbed the steak hammer from the brown pot.

'Hundreds of channels!' shrieked Cato as I swept from the room with the hammer in my hands.

Simon didn't see the steak hammer because he was kneeling on the floor, scouring the television page of the newspaper. Before I had even opened my mouth, Simon turned round and looked me firmly in the eyes. In *his* hands was the remote control. He was pointing it at me. The room didn't smell so bad any more and I noticed he'd lit a real fire with some logs that he must've bought from the Greek shop on his way home; there was something touching about how he'd managed to light a fire without disrupting his viewing pleasure.

For the split second that the remote was aimed at me, I felt myself turned to ice. 'This is Simon,' I thought, and shivered as I realised what was happening. 'Simon's trying to switch me off.' Simon looked so handsome, and so *warm*, in his crumpled office trousers and rolled-up shirtsleeves, his wrists beautiful.

'Why won't you join me?' he said. 'I'm opening a nice bottle of cold white wine in the next break.'

'Ugh,' said Cato from the doorway. I've always loved Simon's wrists and at that moment he was placing the remote control in my hand, as though passing into my care something as delicate as a baby bird.

Simon rolled over to settle another couple of logs on the fire. 'Sit down,' he said. 'It's about to be *The Big Blue*.'

'Probably really embarrassing sex in it,' sniffed Cato.

'I'm sure you'll like it,' said Simon.

'I mean,' said Cato, 'here is a man who spends more time watching sexual content on TV than actually having intercourse.'

'Shush. How would you know a thing like that?' I aimed a friendly poke at Cato with my toe.

Simon looked genuinely hurt. 'Well, it's a guess,' he said. 'I should think I've known you long enough to know what films you like . . .'

Simon turned back to catch the exciting denouement of his favourite property show and I returned the steak hammer to the pot in the kitchen. Cato, meanwhile, manoeuvred himself between Simon and the set. He was all large eyes and drooping whiskers, doing his best imitation of a rescue cat – before it's been rescued. Or perhaps I'd kicked him harder than I'd intended.

'I'm sorry,' I whispered to Cato.

'That's all right,' said Simon, turning to face me. 'So, sit down, before it starts.'

Simon's smile can be quite dazzling in certain lights and firelight's the best.

'Don't fall for it, remember it's the idiot box. It's the life-sucker. Come back to the kitchen,' said Cato, snaking in and out around my legs.

'You don't need the plug-in drug, the tube for boobies,' he said, his tail slippery against the back of my knees.

'Think of the radiation,' he hissed.

But already the screen was filling with a face even more handsome than Simon's.

'Have I never explained about cultural imperialism and the western TV conglomerates?' Cato screeched as Simon squeezed my hand.

'Sshhh, Cato,' I said, sinking into the sofa. Simon adjusted his arm so that my head rested on his shoulder. The fire crackled just enough to let me know it was there. Cato was glaring, quite rudely, at Simon but my eyes had filled with the sudden beauty of the screen so I wasn't looking. I felt Simon kiss the top of my head.

'Oh, ugh,' said Cato. 'I hope he gets a hairball.'

It wasn't perfect: the house was a shambles, the volume of the film a bit louder than I would have liked, but the children would sleep through it. Angus and Ivan were growing into two fine boys. A little warm current of happiness ran through me. It wasn't perfect, but it would do.

Cato had started to sulk, sitting like a picket between me and the television. 'You're just as bad as the rest of them,' he snarled. Then he yawned straight at me so I gave him a little nudge with the side of my foot, and I told him:

'Cato, why don't you go play with a mouse?'

Flick, flick.

Acknowledgements

For generously sharing time and expertise I would like to thank Stephen Carroll-Turner, Leszek Mozdzer, Anna Wloch and Jeremy Young. I am indebted to Nora Ephron for the words of Mary McCarthy taken from her coruscating play *Imaginary Friends*. Lennie Goodings and Ed Victor have been invaluable. I am grateful to Joanna Nelson, Claire Singers and Phil Manzanera and in particular to Charlie Gilmour for lending a hand. Lance and Esther Samson are an inspiration. David Gilmour should be cloned so that every crowded house might have one. Without his support and encouragement I would never find the space.

Also by Polly Samson

LYING IN BED

'Polly Samson has pitched her tales of lopsided love,
ambiguity, jealousy, manipulation and madness perfectly,
and writes with assurance and seduction'
Raffaella Barker

'Stunning, wholly original, by turns dark, clever, witty,
moving. You've read nothing like them. What a debut'
Susan Hill, *Daily Mail*, Books of the Year

'Stylish and truthful . . . quite delicious'
Deborah Moggach

'The sort of prose that makes you miss your bus stop'
Guardian

OUT OF THE PICTURE

Only Lizzie's father – who walked out on her as a child – can answer the questions that haunt her. But betrayed by her stepfather and brutalised by her lover, can she risk any more rejection? This compelling story evokes the heartbreak of childhood loss and the triumphs and disasters in a young woman's search for love and her roots.

'I read it cover to cover in one evening, unable to leave it for long'
Maggie O'Farrell

'Insight, humour and wry sympathy . . . A compelling and moving exploration of the way secrets and lies can breed obsession'
Sunday Times

'She pinpoints the telling detail in character or landscape and brings her prose to life with evocative scents and colours'
Shena McKay, *Daily Telegraph*

**You can order other Virago titles through our website: *www.virago.co.uk*
or by using the order form below**

☐ Lying in Bed   Polly Samson   £7.99

☐ Out of the Picture   Polly Samson   £6.99

*The prices shown above are correct at time of going to press. However, the publishers
reserve the right to increase prices on covers from those previously advertised, without
further notice.*

Please allow for postage and packing: **Free UK delivery.**
Europe: add 25% of retail price; Rest of World: 45% of retail price.

To order any of the above or any other Virago titles, please call our credit
card orderline or fill in this coupon and send/fax it to:

Virago, PO Box 121, Kettering, Northants NN14 4ZQ
Fax: 01832 733076   Tel: 01832 737526
Email: aspenhouse@FSBDial.co.uk

☐ I enclose a UK bank cheque made payable to Virago for £ . . . .
☐ Please charge £ . . . . . . to my Visa/Delta/Maestro

Expiry Date   Maestro Issue No.

NAME (BLOCK LETTERS please) . . . .

ADDRESS . . . .

. . . .

. . . .

Postcode . . . . Telephone . . . .

Signature . . . .

Please allow 28 days for delivery within the UK. Offer subject to price and availability.